Advance P...

THE PRINCE OF STEEL PIER

"An immersive coming-of-age story, beautifully written and full of adventure, that had me cheering for Joey Goodman from the very first page."

—Chris Baron, author of *All of Me* and *The Magical Imperfect*

"Stacy Nockowitz's *The Prince of Steel Pier* has everything a great book needs: an engaging main character, a blooming crush, page-turning adventure, and a loving, quirky family that owns a hotel on the delightfully nostalgic Atlantic City boardwalk. Oh, and don't forget to throw in some just-short-of-too-scary gangsters and a huge helping of heart."

—Nora Raleigh Baskin, award-winning author of *The Truth About My Bat Mitzvah* and *Nine, Ten: A September 11 Story*

"*The Prince of Steel Pier* deftly blends wry insight with deep heart to explore big questions about strength, faith, and power. One of the best middle-grade novels I've ever read!"

—Cindy Baldwin, author of *Where the Watermelons Grow*

"I love the funny voice of Joey/Joseph/Squirt Goodman. (Who wouldn't fall for a Skeeball champion with a big heart and a nervous stomach?) I was captivated by Joey's large lovable family and the authentic rendering of the 1970s Atlantic City setting, complete with gangsters, gangster's daughters, lucky frog fountains, sinister business, and mysterious packages. A fun read from start to finish."

—Gennifer Choldenko, author of the Newbery Honor book *Al Capone Does My Shirts*

THE PRINCE OF STEEL PIER

STACY NOCKOWITZ

KAR-BEN
PUBLISHING

KAR-BEN PUBLISHING®
An imprint of Lerner Publishing Group, Inc.
241 First Avenue North
Minneapolis, MN 55401 USA

Website address: www.karben.com

Cover illustration by Alisha Monnin.
Postcard photo on p. 238 courtesy of the author.

Main body text set in Bembo Std.
Typeface provided by Monotype Typography.

Library of Congress Cataloging-in-Publication Data

Names: Nockowitz, Stacy, author.
Title: The prince of Steel Pier / by Stacy Nockowitz.
Description: Minneapolis, MN : Kar-Ben Publishing, [2022] | Audience: Ages
    10–14. | Audience: Grades 4–6. | Summary: "While helping out at his Jewish
    family's struggling Atlantic City hotel in 1975, thirteen-year-old Joey Goodman gets
    a summer job working for a mobster and faces a life-or-death decision" —Provided
    by publisher.
Identifiers: LCCN 2021035887 | ISBN 9781728430331 (lib. bdg.) |
    ISBN 9781728430348 (pbk.)
Subjects: CYAC: Gangsters—Fiction. | Hotels, motels, etc.—Fiction. | Family-owned
    business enterprises—Fiction. | Jews—New Jersey—Fiction. | Family life—New
    Jersey—Fiction. | Atlantic City (N.J.)—Fiction. | New Jersey—History—20th
    century—Fiction. | LCGFT: Novels.
Classification: LCC PZ7.1.N6265 Pr 2022 | DDC [Fic]—dc23

LC record available at https://lccn.loc.gov/2021035887

Manufactured in the United States of America
1-49484-49528-12/21/2021

FOR MOM, DAD, AND THE
ST. CHARLES IN MY HEART.

CHAPTER 1

ST. BONAVENTURE HOTEL
ATLANTIC CITY, NEW JERSEY

AUGUST 1975

It's nine o'clock on Friday morning, and Mrs. Goldberg is definitely dead.

We stand around the bed in her hotel room, but Mrs. Goldberg isn't waiting for us to decide what to do next. She died in her sleep. She's just lying there, eyes closed, mouth ajar. She's the first dead hotel guest I've ever seen. Come to think of it, she's the first dead anything I've ever seen, except for bugs. That might explain why I'm shaking.

She doesn't look peaceful, like I thought a dead person would look. More like defeated. Or deflated. She's a balloon with the air let out.

Uncle Sol rubs his chin like he expects there to be a beard beneath his fingers. "And here I thought we were going to get through the whole summer without one guest dying on us." The guests at the St. Bonaventure are so old that two or three usually die during the course of a season, but my dad never let me see one before. "Such a shame. Mrs. Goldberg was a good guest. Paid for the whole summer up front. Never missed our Shabbat services."

"She gave good tips too," says my oldest brother, Reuben. "Slipped me an extra ten at the end of August in '73 and '74. She didn't have to do that."

"She looks like a piece of gefilte fish," my other older brother, Simon, mutters.

Dad glares at Simon. "What's the matter with you?"

Simon rolls his eyes. Under his breath, he says, "It's not like she can hear me."

Uh-oh. Whatever's in my stomach starts tossing itself around like a bunch of beanbags.

Uncle Sol turns to my brothers. "Pack her things. I'll go downstairs and make the phone calls." Reuben and Simon begin moving around the room. Simon pulls Mrs. Goldberg's suitcases from the closet, and Reuben starts emptying the dresser drawers.

When Uncle Sol pulls the bedsheet over Mrs. Goldberg's face, I press my hand to my stomach. Why is the room tilting?

Everyone turns and gapes at me.

Oh, wait . . . did I say that out loud?

Dad sighs in his "I knew this would happen" way. He grabs my shoulders and practically pushes me across the room to get me out of there. I notice two dead flies on the carpet by the bathroom threshold. Dead flies and a dead old lady.

A weird, zombie-like groan escapes my throat, and I throw myself at the toilet just in time to puke my guts into the bowl. Perfect. Way to go, Joey. Really impressive. I can't imagine a worse start to my month down here at the shore.

Someone puts a hand on my back. "You okay, squirt?" It's Reuben. "Too much for you, huh?"

I answer him by barfing some more.

When I'm sure I've emptied myself out completely, I squeeze into the space between the toilet and the tub. I swipe at my face with my shirt sleeve. Great. Shaking, throwing up, *and* crying.

My eyes float over a framed picture on the wall across from where I'm huddled. It's an old, colorful print of Steel Pier and the Boardwalk and the beach back in the '30s or '40s, back when Atlantic City was the most popular vacation spot in the country. The sky in the poster is the color of robins' eggs, and I press my lips together hard, thinking I'll never again see the sky that blue, the sand that clean, Steel Pier that golden and glowing. Once you've seen a dead body, things don't look that perfect anymore.

★ ★ ★

No other guests die over the weekend, but my whole family still tiptoes around me like I'm a hospital patient. They whisper in corners, thinking I can't hear them, but if there's one thing about us Jews, it's that we're not quiet people.

Mom keeps putting her hands on her cheeks and shaking her head. "He could be traumatized for life!" Then she grouches at Dad for bringing me up to Mrs. Goldberg's room.

Bubbe and Zeyde, my grandmother and grandfather, keep telling me to go lie down. That's their response to everything. Skin your knee? "Go lie down." Have a rash? "Go lie down."

At least five times, Reuben says, "I could take him for a slice of pizza."

Uncle Sol thinks he's a doctor. "Give him flat ginger ale. That will settle his stomach."

Even my ten-year-old brother, Ben, has something to say about the whole thing. "I coulda told you that Joey was gonna upchuck when he saw the dead lady. When the next guest dies, I'm going to go look at the body. It'll be good for my acting. Maybe the next part I get will be as a corpse." He rolls his eyes back and dangles his tongue out of the corner of his mouth.

Here's what nobody says: "It's okay, Joey. We know there's a strong, coolheaded guy inside of you somewhere!" Nope. No one says that.

By Monday, I've had it with the adults' nervous glances and Simon's annoying jokes ("Hey, Joey, what's up? Oh, it's your breakfast!"). I'm more than ready to leave my grandparents' house in Margate, which my parents and my brothers and I take over for the month of August, and go back to my nonpaying job as a waiter-in-training at the hotel.

I work the breakfast shift in the dining room with Reuben and Simon. They're seventeen and sixteen, so they're real waiters. They talk to the guests; I assist. This basically means I follow them around the dining room and pick up all the stuff that the guests drop on the floor. The dining room empties out by nine thirty. The guests go off to do whatever it is old Jewish people do in Atlantic City. They'll all be back for lunch at noon on the dot. I don't have to work until the dinner shift, so I have the whole day stretching out in front of me. It's time to get out of here and hit the arcade.

Which means I need some money.

I swing through the lobby, over the scuffed black-and-white tile floor, and past the round, stone fountain with the four ceramic frogs shooting water out of their upturned mouths. I rub one of the frogs' heads, like I always do, and approach the front desk. Uncle Sol is there working with an adding machine and a ledger. His fingers fly across the keys, and the printed tape spills over the counter and curls in on itself like a ribbon on a present. He wears a red sports jacket and a dark blue tie, so he looks kind of like the guy who does the play-by-play for the Phillies games on TV. A pin on his lapel announces him: *Solomon Broder, General Manager.*

Here we go. Uncle Sol and I fall into the same routine every August. Sometimes he ends up giving me some money, and sometimes he doesn't. But we always start with small talk. I dread this.

"Uncle Sol?"

He glances up for a moment, then returns to his calculations. "Yes, Joey?"

I'm going to ask him some questions I already have the answers to. "Uncle Sol, do you know where my dad is?" It's Monday. Dad's at work back in Philadelphia, which is where we Goodmans live eleven months of the year. In August, when the rest of us are helping out at the hotel, Dad goes to work from Monday through Thursday, and then he joins the rest of us down the shore for the weekend.

"He's at work, Joey. It's Monday." Uncle Sol's shirt is too tight, and I watch his potbelly expand and contract with his breathing.

"Oh, right. I knew that." I pick at some pretend lint on my shirt. Then, "You know where my mom is?" Mom's not here either. She drove Ben to Philly for a TV commercial audition.

He narrows his eyes at me over his glasses, like he's thinking. Even though we both know that we both know the answer. "She took Benjamin to an audition. She'll be back later." Then he gives me his "I'm trying to be patient with you" look. Our shtick is in full swing now. "Joey, do you need some money?"

I pull my kippah off my head and scratch at my mop of curly black hair just to have something to do. "Maybe a little. You know, for the arcade? Skee-Ball or something?"

I know what comes next, and I brace for it.

"Money doesn't grow on trees, you know." Uncle Sol stops pecking at the adding machine. He leans across the front desk on his elbows so his face is close to mine. "The arcade is a waste of money. You know that, right? No return on the investment."

I chew my bottom lip for a moment. "I win lots of prize tickets, though. If I win enough of them, I'll be able to get a really good prize."

He shakes his head slowly. "Like what? Those prizes are all junk."

Uncle Sol isn't married, and he doesn't have any kids. Dad says, "Sol has plenty of money to keep him warm at night," but my uncle has lonely eyes. If he wants to act like he's my father every once in a while, I don't mind it so much.

"I really want a camera," I tell him. "I can get a Kodak Instamatic if I win ten thousand prize tickets."

"And how much money do you end up spending to win all those tickets? Did you ever think about that? What do you want a camera for, anyway? I didn't have a camera until I was thirty years old."

This conversation is going south quickly. I don't have much of an answer for him. I want a camera because I want to take pictures of stuff—my friends and baseball games and bugs and nature. It just seems like a cool thing to do. But *cool* is not a concept my uncle understands. Looks like this is going to be one of those times when I walk away without a cent.

But in an unexpected turn of events, Uncle Sol reaches into his inside jacket pocket and pulls out his billfold. His brow is wrinkled, as if he wants me to know how troubling this decision is for him. He takes out a ten-dollar bill and displays it for me, holding it with his thumbs and index fingers. "This ten has to last you all week, Joey. And you should think about putting some of it aside if you really want to buy a camera." Uncle Sol would be a good Jewish parent. He really knows how to lay on the guilt.

I nod. "Thanks, Uncle Sol." And he hands me the ten.

An old man with wisps of powder-white hair appears beside me. "The television in our room isn't working right." He has a thick accent, Russian or Polish, like a lot of the guests. "My wife can't watch her stories in the afternoon if the television doesn't work."

Uncle Sol turns his attention to the guest, and I back away from the front desk, the ten-dollar bill heavy in my hand.

But at least that scene is over. Now I have ten bucks, and I'm free for six hours.

The Boardwalk is mostly empty at this time of day. The tourists will start dribbling out onto the boards soon with their gargantuan ice cream cones and their sunburned shoulders. But for now, it's just me, a bunch of local boys throwing clumsy karate kicks at each other outside of Woolworth's, and the disinterested seagulls. I have my favorite book, *The Once and Future King* by T. H. White, in one hand and a grocery bag full of my arcade prize tickets in the other hand. I've changed into a tank top and shorts, but I'm sweating up a storm just putting one foot in front of the other. I think they said on the radio that it's going to top a hundred degrees today. I already want a soda.

To get out of this heat, I plan on stepping into every third or fourth storefront and soaking up the air-conditioning. I go into a big sundry store first, and the guy behind the cash register watches me meander up and down the aisles. He leans his body over so I stay in his line of sight as I go from section to section. I put my head down at first, but that might make me look like I'm going to shoplift something, so I end up concentrating too hard on stuff on the shelves in front of me. Now I look like I'm overly interested in suntan lotion.

The guy up front is wearing one of those short-sleeved, button-down jacket things like a pharmacist wears, and he's got his hands shoved in the pockets. He has empty eyes, a long, sunken face, and a needle-thin mustache. If I saw him on the street, I'd probably think *he's* a shoplifter. That or a murderer. He musters every ounce of energy he has just to watch me wander around, and I wonder if he's hiding a knife or something in those pockets.

I go rigid when I hear his creepy, low-pitched voice. "You gonna buy something or what, kid?"

This day is off to a very shaky start. I draw in a deep breath and approach the counter. "Got any cold soda?"

With his chin, he indicates a refrigerator case to his left. All they have in the case is Fanta. I don't drink Fanta because Uncle Sol says it was invented by the Nazis, but I have no choice at this point. I'm fully committed to buying a bottle of soda in this store now. I sigh and stare at my options: Fanta Grape or Fanta Orange. Does it matter which one I pick? I grab the closest bottle, and Uncle Sol's face flashes across my mind. He's wincing.

When I give the guy the ten-dollar bill, he mutters, "Got anything smaller than a ten?" He mumbles like we're doing something illegal. He's got a cigarette burned almost to the filter sitting in a little blue ashtray next to the cash register. A reed of smoke curls through the air and into my nose. A cough tries to escape, but I shut my mouth tight and just shake my head. He squints at me. "Where'd you get a bill this big?" he asks. "Did you steal this ten?"

I blink at him. I just want my change. And now I need to use the bathroom. "I didn't steal it. My uncle gave it to me. At the St. Bonaventure, a couple doors down. My grandparents own the hotel." He raises one eyebrow. "Well, my grandparents and my uncle. The one who gave me the ten." Where did that come from? Why am I telling this weird guy my life story?

My open palm hovers in the air between us. He takes his sweet time fishing in the register for my change. "I know about that hotel. That's the Jew hotel." He puts the bills on the counter instead of in my hand and drops the coins on top of them.

For a moment, the air around us is completely still. I force myself to stare right back into his lifeless eyes, and I think we'll be locked like that forever. He crosses his arms over his scrawny chest and sneers at me. He doesn't even want our hands to touch accidentally. Finally, I sweep my change into my bag of tickets. I leave the bottle of soda on the counter and walk out.

Back on the Boardwalk, I shake with anger. *That's the Jew hotel.* His words twist through my body and settle in the pit of my stomach, and I know I'll never forget them for the rest of my life. He said them to me, but it was like he was saying them to my whole family, my people. If he'd said that to Simon, Simon would've stood up to him. Maybe I should go back in there and confront him. *Yeah, it's a Jew hotel, and I'm one of the Jews from that hotel! What about it?* But I don't go back in. I only say those things inside my head.

All I can do now is start moving my feet toward the arcade again.

A block or two down, I duck into a little luncheonette. I've never been in this place, but I really need to use the bathroom. Inside, red vinyl stools line the counter on the right, and booths sit back-to-back on the left down the length of the restaurant. Only one booth is taken. Two muscular men who can barely fit in the booth sit across from a tall man with a mustache and a thin, well-dressed man with a dark red tie. The two beefy guys have their shirtsleeves rolled up to reveal their fleshy forearms. Empty plates are scattered across the table, and the men are all drinking coffee and smoking. They look like they've been here since last week.

"What can I get you, sweetie?" a waitress behind the counter calls out to me. A pin on her chest says ANITA in crooked, black letters. Her wrinkled skin flaps all over as she wipes down the counter.

"Can I just use the restroom?" I'm pretty sure she's going to tell me I have to buy something first.

But she must notice me fidgeting because she says, "Sure, honey. It's around the back to the right."

The bathroom isn't big enough for me to turn around twice, and the floor looks kind of damp and sticky, so I double back and leave my book and my bag on the end of the counter before I go in and shut the door. I try to get the lock to work, but the doorknob is so loose that I'm afraid I'm going to pull it off the door altogether. I go really quickly, praying that no one opens the door while my shorts are pulled down.

When I step out of the bathroom, my book is still on the counter where I left it, but my bag of prize tickets is gone.

I must have four or five hundred tickets in that bag, tickets that I won playing Skee-Ball since we came down the shore at the beginning of August. And the bag has my money in it. It's not a ton of money, just $9.50 now, but it's money that Uncle Sol gave to me, trusted me with. I look around, hoping maybe the bag fell on the floor, but of course it's not on the floor. I grip the edge of the counter hard. Dread is seeping in through my pores, pulsing at my temple.

"Excuse me!" I blurt out to Anita. She comes over and gives me a tired smile. "Did you happen to see the bag that I put up here on the counter with my book?"

Anita tilts her head back so I can look over her shoulder. And there's my bag, sitting right on the table of the only occupied booth in the place. The two huge men facing me are chatting away, laughing and sucking on their cigarettes, as if they're relaxing in their own kitchen. "Sorry, kid," she says, and she does sound sorry. Sorry and weary, like she pities me.

I grab my book off the counter and stand there, rooted to the floor. I don't know what I'm going to do now. All I know is that it's my bag, and they took it. I don't even realize that I'm making a decision until I approach the booth. I stop in front of the four men. Their conversation trails off, and they all turn their heads to me at once. Their cigarettes hang off their lips.

The man to my left squints at me. "What do you want?" he says. Pastry crumbs stick to the corners of his mouth, and he's got a few hairs dangling out of his nostrils.

My mouth is dry as paper. "That's my bag. I want it back."

The three big guys shoot one another a look like they can't believe I spoke to them, and they start laughing. The fourth man, the one with the red tie, watches me with calm, dark eyes.

Nose Hairs gives me an exaggerated shrug. "I don't see no bag, kid." His friends keep chuckling. His hands are as big as softballs.

"That bag right on the table," I say, as if he really doesn't know what bag I'm talking about.

He looks at it like it just materialized out of thin air. "Oh, you mean *this* bag? Oh, that's *my* bag." Nobody is laughing anymore.

Oh, no. No, no, no. I need to leave right now. I need to walk away.

But I hear myself say, "No, it's not. It's mine."

"I don't see no name on that bag. What makes you think it's yours?" He sucks his teeth with a high-pitched squeak. One of his pals starts drumming his knuckles on the table, and I picture them doing the same on my head.

My courage empties out of me like water down a drain. I feel my jaw hang open, but the words have left me too.

The thin man in the corner of the booth says, "Ralphie, give the kid his bag."

Ralphie stares at me for a few more seconds. But finally his face eases into a grin. He and the other men start laughing again, and Ralphie's meaty hand grabs my arm. I flinch, but he's not letting go. "I'm just kiddin' with ya, kid! What, you can't take a joke? Here. Here's your bag." He hands it to me, and I clutch it hard so he can't see my hand shaking. "You're a tough kid. Here . . ." He lets go of my arm, rolls his body to the left, and reaches into his right pant pocket. "Take this." He slaps a twenty-dollar bill on the table.

I glance at the thin man, and he nods, like he's giving me permission to take the money. "No, thanks," I say, and I slip my book into the bag and turn to leave. But Ralphie grabs my arm again and clenches it more firmly than before.

His smile is tight, and his eyes are glassy blue. "You don't want to insult me now, do you? Be a good sport. Take the money."

I don't understand what's happening. Does he *want* me to take this money or is he *daring* me to? The four of them watch me, and the tall guy across from Ralphie curls his lip up in a creepy grin. He exhales cigarette smoke out of his nose, and it hovers over the table.

I don't know why, but I look to the thin man in the

suit. He nods at me again. "Go ahead," he says. "You earned it."

I have no idea what he's talking about. How did I earn it? At this point, though, I don't think Ralphie's letting go of my arm until I take the money, so I reach for the twenty on the table and drop it in the grocery bag. As soon as I do this, the four of them start chuckling again like this is some comedy act. Somehow that twenty weighs down the bag like river rocks. Ralphie finally lets go of me, and I know I've been dismissed.

The walk to the door is a thousand feet long. The sun pours through the door's glass, and I squint hard against the glare. It's like I'm stepping out of a cave after a long sleep. I barely get onto the Boardwalk before I feel vomit burning the back of my throat. I sprint to the closest garbage can.

CHAPTER 2

With my head almost touching the metal rim of the garbage can, a disgusting mixture of odors clobbers me. Cigarette butts, ketchup, fruit punch. At my feet, pigeons peck at scraps of bread that have fallen to the Boardwalk. In no time, my breakfast comes right up.

I tremble as I lean over the can. I honestly didn't think I could throw up this much in the course of just a few days. Mrs. Goldberg's dead face swims behind my eyelids. The big guy in the diner, Ralphie, called me tough. Me, Joey Goodman? Tough? My brother Simon would howl with laughter at that idea. Especially if he saw me now. My family could tell Ralphie story after story that would get that idea right out of his head.

When I finish unloading everything in my stomach, I shuffle like an old man over to a bench that looks out on the beach and the ocean beyond. My breath comes in little skips through my nose.

Bubbe says that I don't pray enough, and that's why I get so anxious about everything—because I don't let God guide me. But lately, I have to remind myself an awful lot to believe in God. I never doubted God's existence when I was a little kid. Why would I? My parents and my grandparents and my teachers all told me God was there, and I believed them.

But then I turned twelve. I started studying for my bar mitzvah and learning what all those Hebrew prayers we say really mean, and everything became blurry. I asked my dad why God would let so much terrible stuff happen to the Jews, to us, His people. Dad told me that it was complicated and that I should go talk to Rabbi Kahn. But I thought the rabbi might get mad at me for doubting God, so I never asked. I've been pretty confused ever since. I went through with my bar mitzvah this past March, of course, and I said all the right words, but I don't know if I meant them. And that scares me because how can I really be Jewish if I don't believe in God? And if I'm not Jewish, I don't know who I am.

It's too hot to sit out here like a walrus on a rock. I cancel the arcade mission for the time being. I'm almost too heat-whipped to stand, but I manage, and I point myself in the direction of the St. Bonaventure. Maybe I can convince Reuben to let me work the lunch shift with him. Anything to strip my mind of all that's happened this morning.

If God is up there, I wonder what He has lined up for me next.

A few days pass, and I don't touch the twenty that guy Ralphie gave me. It's hiding somewhere in my bag of prize tickets like a virus, contaminating the $9.50 left from Uncle Sol's ten. I wonder what God would like me to do with that twenty. Maybe it's a test. *Will you spend it or not, Joey?* God may be waiting for that answer before He makes His presence known to me. Or Her presence. God could be a woman. Actually, if Bubbe is any indication of what it's like with a woman in charge, God probably *is* a woman.

Ben landed the commercial he auditioned for on Monday, and he's celebrating by entertaining guests in the lobby with some show tunes. The old people clap along to Ben's a cappella songs. Everyone is smiling— everyone except Mom, who lets out a little gasp whenever Ben comes close to slipping on the carpet or falling against the fountain. "He'll crack his head open!" I hear her pained whisper to Reuben, who slides his arm around her shoulder and shushes her. She quiets down but watches Ben like he's about to run into traffic.

Uncle Sol and a gray-haired man in a slick suit stand behind the front desk. The guy in the suit is doing a lot of talking with his hands. He points to an amber-colored water stain the size of a catcher's mitt on the ceiling and then to a long, winding crack in the lobby's floor tiles. My uncle's back is stiff as a board, and his mouth is tight. Why is that guy even here? When the man shakes his hand and walks off toward the Boardwalk entrance, my uncle sighs and rubs his neck.

I reach into a candy dish on a side table and pop a saltwater taffy in my mouth. Zeyde, who's standing next to me, does the same. "Don't tell your bubbe," he says to me. He pretends to button his lips closed. He takes a tissue from his pocket and cleans his glasses. "I have to go fix a few shower leaks. Would you like to help me?" Zeyde can fix anything. Sometimes, I go on his rounds with him and hand him a wrench or a screwdriver when he needs it.

"I was going to go play some Skee-Ball, Zeyde. But I'll come with you next time, okay?"

Zeyde shrugs. "Sure, go! Go play your game. The list of what needs fixing around here isn't going to get any shorter." He moves his eyes around the ceiling until they land on a different water stain in a corner. I see it too, and I wish I hadn't. Are there any prayers to say for an aging hotel? My heart twists. It's the same feeling I get when I look at Zeyde sometimes, when I realize that he's getting old and there's nothing I can do about it.

My lungs can't take in any more of the stale air in here. It's like I'm breathing in oldness. I'll feel much better when I get to the arcade. I'm so calm when I'm playing Skee-Ball. Why can't Skee-Ball be a religion? At least I know I'd be doing it right.

* * *

It's more crowded on the Boardwalk this afternoon than it was when I was out here a few days ago. Bag and book in hand, I bob and weave like a boxer among the tourists, looking for my openings so I bump into as few people as possible. When I get close to that sundry store, the one with the undead cashier, my pace quickens. It's not like the guy can feel my presence through the walls or anything. I just don't want to take a chance that he might be looking out the window as I pass. My stomach drops and my heart pounds until the store is well behind me.

I reach Pinky's, a place with an arcade up front and a restaurant with a bar in the back. It's not the best choice for a thirteen-year-old kid on his own. I mean, I've never heard of anybody getting knifed there or anything, but you never know with some of these shady characters that populate Atlantic City nowadays. The Boardwalk used to be such a friendly, safe place. Dad used to take my brothers and me to shake hands with Mr. Peanut outside the Planter's store. We'd go to Steel Pier at sunset and ride the Sky Wheel ten times in a row. Not anymore. Now, an evening at Steel Pier could be dangerous.

But it's only one in the afternoon right now, so Pinky's it is.

Inside, the AC is loud as a buzz saw, much louder than it ought to be, considering it's belching out warmish air. A couple of older teenage boys with long hair are playing pinball. They move and jerk as they play, as if their body motions can will the little silver ball to hit the bonus bumpers. When one of the boys loses, he slams a hand on the glass top of his machine, and I jump.

"You bang on the glass like that again and you're out of here!" the bald guy behind the prize counter yells. He turns his attention to a little girl with a fistful of tickets, and the teenager playing pinball repeats everything the man said in a snarky, nasal voice. The boy at the other machine snorts but doesn't take his eyes off his flippers. These two may be obnoxious, but they're not scary enough to make me leave, not when Skee-Ball is so very close.

Since the back half of this place is a bar and restaurant, the arcade area up front is small. There are only four Skee-Ball alleys. I slip a five into the change machine, and it pukes up twenty quarters for me. I dump them in my ticket bag and choose the alley on the end, closest to the low wall that separates the arcade from the bar. I place my book and my bag of tickets on the floor between my feet where no one can get to them. I insert a quarter in the coin slot on the front of the machine and push the red button to release the polished wood balls down the channel to my right.

I start my first game, and pretty soon I'm in a rhythm. *Swing* my arm back, then forward and *release!* The ball *roooollllls* up the ramp and . . . *jumps!* Then it missiles into a hole in the board at the end of the alley. The machine spits out ribbons of tickets that make a heaping pile on the floor. I must have fifty or sixty tickets next to me in the course of an hour or so.

I'm not paying the least attention to the people coming and going, so I startle when I hear: "Hey, it's the kid from the diner! Little tough guy!"

Oh, no. I recognize the voice immediately, and my stomach seizes. I swing my head around, and there's my friend Ralphie, big as a bear, barreling toward me, his two Neanderthal friends right behind him. They look like they've grown since I saw them in the diner a few days ago. Or maybe it's just seeing them standing up that shocks me.

Where's the smaller man, the one who seemed to be in charge of these guys?

In two seconds, they tower over me like Godzilla and a couple of his Tokyo-wrecking pals. Grinning, Ralphie grabs me by my upper arms and lifts me off my feet. "You remember this kid?" he asks the other two before depositing me back on the tile. They nod and grunt. He points at the floor. "That's *our* bag, right, kid?" He snickers at his own little joke.

The burly one next to Ralphie eyes my mound of tickets coming out of the Skee-Ball machine, which puts me on high alert. He nudges Ralphie and says, "Look at all those tickets! He's gotta be cheating. I like this kid!" The strands of brown hair he has left are combed way over his head from above his ear.

Ralphie bends down so we're eye to eye. "What's your name, kid?"

"Joey." I manage to raise my voice enough to be heard. He's got circles of sweat under his arms. His whole being looks damp.

Ralphie glances at the other two. "Kid's name is Joey." Back to me. "Joey what?"

"Goodman," I say, a little stronger this time.

Comb-over hangs his arm off of Ralphie's shoulder. "And are you a *good man*?" he asks, raising his eyebrows like he's very clever, like he's the first person to come up with that one.

"Yeah!" Oh, man, that did not come out right. It's only because I'm scared witless, but I just yelled at them.

All three men do some variation on "Ooooh!" and glance at one another like I spoke back to a teacher and I'm about to be sent to the principal's office.

"See, Grunts?" Ralphie says to the third man. "I told you he was a tough kid!"

The guy's nickname is a perfect fit. Grunts responds, but I can't understand a word he says.

A smooth voice drifts up to us. "Can't you three leave this kid alone?" They turn around and I see him, the suave guy from the diner. For no real reason, relief floods through my whole body. He looks like he's air-conditioned from the inside out, not a wrinkle or sweat stain on his yellow dress shirt. This time his tie is striped in shades of green. With his dark hair slicked back and his tan suit jacket slung over his shoulder, he could be a movie star. They part to let him come through, toward me. "They bothering you, kid?" he asks.

I don't know how to answer that question. All I know is I don't want to make these guys mad. "Not really," I reply. This must be a decent answer because the man smiles at me and nods. Then the smile is gone as quickly as it came.

"Your parents know you're in this place?" He gestures around him. Where's he going with this? Am I about to be kidnapped?

I stammer out my answer. "I—I just want to play Skee-Ball."

He points to my pile of tickets on the floor. "You must be pretty good at Skee-Ball, winning all those tickets." He turns to Comb-over. "Eddie, why don't you count the kid's tickets for him?"

"Count the tickets?" asks Comb-over, aka Eddie. He looks as confused as I feel.

"Yes, Eddie," the thin man says. "Count the kid's tickets."

The corner of Eddie's mouth twitches. He shuffles his king-size body over to the Skee-Ball alley next to mine and sags down on the end of the ramp. With great effort, he leans over to pick up my prize tickets from the floor. He begins counting them out loud but settles into just moving his lips.

The well-dressed man places his jacket over the back of a nearby folding chair and says to me, "So are you? Any good?"

I shrug. "I'm pretty good." I'm being modest. I could go pro.

Ralphie says, "I was watching him, Artie. The kid's great." This is completely untrue. He hasn't seen me roll a single ball. I don't point this out. "His name's Joey, Joey Goodman."

To me he asks, "You know who this is, right?" He claps the thin man's shoulder. I shake my head. Ralphie squints at me like he just watched me eat something weird. "You serious, kid? This is Artie Bishop. *The* Artie Bishop!"

From his expression, I can see that I'm supposed to be impressed, so I nod and say, "Oh, okay." I move my eyes back and forth between them and try to radiate sincerity.

Artie juts his chin out toward me. "So, Joey, let's see your skills."

"What do you mean? You want to watch me play Skee-Ball?" That can't be what he means.

"Seventy-two!" From my right, Eddie's shout jolts me. He gathers the tickets together and dumps them into my grocery bag.

Artie nods. "Go ahead," he says to me. "I'll give you five bucks if you get a hundred points with one ball."

What am I, God's punching bag? There is no Jewish prayer for this situation. "O-Only one ball?"

It's nearly impossible to get a hundred points with one ball. The hundred-point holes are barely big enough for the ball to go in, and you have to roll it perfectly to get it to jump into that tiny hole. I mean, I've done it, sure—plenty of times. But usually I don't risk wasting the ball.

And what if I miss? Then what? Ralphie's practically panting with anticipation. Grunts raises one bushy eyebrow at me. The four of them hover over me, sucking the air directly out of my lungs.

I can't believe I'm doing this, but I say, "Okay." Sweat coats my back. "I just—I need some space."

Artie spreads his arms out, herding the other three men like giant sheep, so they move back a few feet. "Go ahead, kid."

Before I can even turn around to face the Skee-Ball alley, Ralphie blurts out, "Hey, Eddie, I'll bet you twenty he makes it!"

"I'll take that action," Eddie replies, and he rubs his hands together. "Twenty he blows it."

I don't think my insides can take this.

Artie steps toward me and puts his hand on my shoulder. His gaze holds me. "Don't worry about them. They're not the enemy right now. That machine is. I have faith in you, kid. Just go on. Get that hundred." He steps back. He has faith in me? Why?

I tingle with adrenaline from my hair down to my toes. I turn toward the Skee-Ball alley and reach down into the slot where the wooden balls sit. I move the ball around in my hands until I grip it just like I want to. I take a deep, deep breath.

I wind my arm back, thrust it forward, and release the ball into the alley. Ralphie and Eddie are behind me, yelling, "Go, go, go!" and "Miss it! Miss it!" The ball speeds up the ramp. At the end of the alley, the ball jumps up, and I swear it stops right there, in midair! I crush my eyes closed because I don't want to know.

The machine dings. Ralphie shouts in triumph. I look

up at the score display, and it has added a hundred points to my total. I moan with relief. When I spin around, Artie grins and nods at me. Ralphie has his arms thrust high in the air, and he's laughing and whooping. Eddie shakes his head, and he rips a twenty from the wad of bills he takes from his pocket. I smile at Artie like he's my dad. He hands me five bucks, which I know I've earned, and I fold it up before flipping it into my bag of tickets.

Ralphie shoves a few ones into my hand. "I knew you could do it, Joey Good-man! That's your cut of the winnings." He pats my cheek a couple of times.

"You must be cheating, kid," Eddie says. "I don't know how you did that."

Ralphie pushes him in his shoulder. "Another twenty says he does it again!" He points to me and asks, "You could do it again, right, kid?"

"I don't know." Because I don't know if I could ever do that again. Certainly not right now.

"No way he can get a hundred twice in a row," Eddie says.

"I think he can do it." A voice comes over the half-wall separating the arcade from the bar. A redheaded woman in a pink blouse and thick pink lipstick stands on the bar side of the wall. "Come on, Eddie," she adds. "Twenty for me too."

Eddie nods. "You got it, Lil."

I look to Artie. "I don't think I can—"

He shakes his finger at me. "Faith, Joey." To the woman, Lil, he says, "He'll make it." *I will?* I don't think Artie and I have the same definition of faith.

"Go on, kid," Eddie says. "I want my money back."

Artie winks at me. Something in me doesn't want to let him down. I grab another wooden ball from the slot and let it roll. This time I watch it sail right into the hundred-point hole, and I jump in excitement. Ralphie and Lil cheer for me, while Eddie slaps his forehead in disbelief. I'm as stunned as he is.

Grunts takes one of the balls from the slot and holds it in the air, examining it like a scientist looking at a test tube. What does he think he's going to find? As my dad would say, these guys aren't the sharpest pencils in the drawer. Ralphie and Eddie egg each other on like six-year-olds. At one point, I think I hear them get into a "Nuh-uh!"/"Uh-huh!" exchange.

Lil calls people over from the bar. They set their drinks on top of the half-wall, and Lil tells them very exaggerated things about my Skee-Ball skills. I shake some hands, smile, introduce myself. It's like I'm running for office.

People talk across me, over me. Ralphie is my new best friend. He hands me more money and puts his arm around my shoulder. "Fifty bucks says he gets five hundred points in the next game!" he shouts to the room, and before I know what's happened, they're all calling bets—for me, against me. Ralphie leans over and mutters in my ear, "Don't do too good, okay? The crowd needs a show." He dips his head and gives me an exaggerated wink.

A show? Didn't this guy just bet money on me? Then it dawns on me: he wants me to lose a little, to get behind in my score so he can up the bets. Maybe Ralphie's smarter than I thought. My heart is going a thousand miles a minute. I look over at Artie, but his attention is no longer on me. I follow his gaze to the floor, where my bag sits.

I go very still. Does he want my tickets? My money? Why would he want either? I swipe at my mouth with the back of my hand and watch Artie reach down toward my bag. But it's not the bag he wants; it's the book. He picks up *The Once and Future King* and turns it over in his hands. He steps back from the group and starts reading the back cover intently, tuning out the chatter and noise around him.

I'm drawn back in when I hear "Don't let me down, Joey!" A woman with long, feathered blonde hair elbows the man next to her.

A bald guy offers me his drink. "Here, kid, have a sip of this! Should throw your game off but good!" And he laughs like a hyena.

Lil pulls his arm back. "You shouldn't bet against him, Mickey!"

I drop a quarter in the front of the machine, and twelve balls roll down the slot toward me. I lick my lips and take a very deep breath, like the deepest breath I've ever taken. Then I let the balls fly. Fifty points. Forty points. Fifty points. Each time I pick up a ball, everyone quiets down, and they lean forward in anticipation. As soon as the ball goes in a hole, they erupt in a roar. I throw in a couple of thirty-pointers, like Ralphie said, and even a twenty, just to keep it interesting.

More people from the bar crowd around, wanting to see what all the noise is about. People make side bets on individual rolls, and money passes around like notes in science class. This is amazing! Electric energy pounds in my veins. I hop from foot to foot, shake my hands out, exhale with a hoot.

I'm at 460 points with one ball left. I dry my hands off on my shorts and pick up the last ball. My faith kicks in, all right, my Skee-Ball faith. I concentrate on the board. The forty-point hole expands until it's the size of a manhole. And I make the ball soar.

I don't even have to look to know where it landed.

Pandemonium erupts around me. Ralphie lets out a whoop of joy. He lifts me off my feet and spins me around. People are handing me money left and right.

Men clap my shoulders and women kiss my cheeks. I'm sweating so much that I may melt into the floor. Someone hands me a bottle of Coke, and I chug it down so fast that my eyes water.

The crowd finally clears out. Eddie, Ralphie, and Grunts join their friends by the bar, and people return to their tables. The noise dissolves into a normal hum. I rip the prize tickets from the slot on the Skee-Ball machine and toss them into my bag along with all the money people shoved at me, a pile that seems too thick to count. Artie sits in the folding chair where he placed his jacket, still as a statue, reading *The Once and Future King*. Something in his posture tells me he's been reading it this whole time, which is pretty cool. When he finally looks up, he smiles at me and rises from the chair.

"You like this book?" he asks. "You had it with you in the diner too."

"It's my favorite book."

He runs his hand over the front cover. "I'll tell you what, Joey, I'm going to keep this book for a few days so I can finish it. Come back and see me here on Saturday, and we'll talk about it. Sound good?"

Yes! Yes! I want to scream. But . . . how am I going to get back here on Saturday? The Shabbat crowd in the dining room at the hotel lingers over every meal for hours. Still, I want to find a way to be here. No one has ever wanted to discuss *The Once and Future King* with me. I doubt my family has even noticed me reading it. I *will* find a way to be here. So I say, "Sure. What time should I come by?"

Artie plucks his jacket from the back of the chair. "Come in around noon. And, Joey, you did real good today. You're tough as nails, kid." And he strolls away, toward the bar. I let out a little giggle, but then I feel ridiculous, so I cover it up with a fake cough. I push out the door, and the bells and dings of the arcade follow me onto the Boardwalk.

Back on the boards, I'm lightheaded. Everything hurts—my arm, my ribs, my back. But I feel fantastic. I could leap over a building like Superman! I have more than enough money to buy that Kodak Instamatic now!

I can't stop smiling as I start back toward the St. Bonaventure. I have no idea what time it is, and I don't care. If I'm late for the dinner shift, I'll just have to explain where I've been, and what happened, and . . .

Wait. What am I thinking? I can't tell my family about this! What would I say? "Hey, Mom, Uncle Sol, Bubbe! I just won some money at a bar playing Skee-Ball for a bunch of shifty guys who don't seem to have day jobs"? I might be able to tell Reuben, *maybe*, but I'm not even 100 percent sure on that. I definitely can't waltz right out and buy a camera with this money. If my parents or grandparents find out about this, I'll be in serious trouble. They'll probably make me give all the money back! I practically choke thinking how humiliating it would be. Ralphie might even be insulted, and then what would happen?

I snap back to reality. I'm on the Boardwalk. It's Thursday afternoon. I haven't said a word to anyone yet. I open the bag just enough to get a glimpse of what's inside. My eyes sweep over the bills—so many bills—and I snap the bag shut. I run my hand over the outside of it, checking for any little holes or tears. The quarters have all settled at the bottom, and I'm concerned about them breaking the bag. So I make a little basket with the hem of my tank top and place the bag in it. I cross my arm over the whole bulky mess and head for the hotel. Now I have to figure out how I'm going to hide this money from my family until the end of the month.

CHAPTER 3

Back at the hotel, I make a beeline for the men's room in the far corner of the ballroom. It's as isolated a spot as any in this old place. I doubt the bathrooms back here have been redone since the St. Bonaventure opened fifty years ago, in 1925. I pull on one of the wooden stall doors, and the hinges squeak like I'm in a haunted house. I freeze and hold my breath. When I'm sure the coast is clear, I go in and lock the door.

The toilet has a wooden seat and cover with one of those pull chains to flush it. I unroll my shirt and place the bag on the toilet cover. I think I've worked out a way to hide the money, but I want to count it first. The bills are a crumpled mess, so I take each one out individually and press it flat against the toilet cover. I start counting.

One hundred and twenty-seven dollars.

"Oh, yeah!" I say aloud. It's the most money I've ever held in my life. I made some money at my bar mitzvah back in March, but Mom and Dad took it and put all of it into a bank account. I never actually saw it. This money is more real than the checks in the envelopes people slipped me at the bar mitzvah. If I can see it and hold it, then I can be sure of it, like holding a picture in my hands.

The problem with this very real pile of money in my hands is that no one is ever supposed to know I have it, so it'll be pretty tricky to spend it. I can't buy a camera with money only I know exists. I shove that thought away for now, though.

I fold the pile in half and push it inside my tube sock, all the way down to where you can't see it against the inside of my sneaker. It's incredibly uncomfortable, but this is how I'll get it back to my grandparents' house. I think I know the perfect place to hide it there, somewhere no one would think to look. I impress myself with this foolproof plan. Now I can just walk into the lobby or the dining room or wherever with my regular old bag of prize tickets and quarters. My family won't suspect a thing. I leave the ballroom whistling and bopping to my off-key tune.

I turn a corner and plow straight into my mother. Ben lopes behind her. They must have just come from the pool. Mom's wearing her terry cloth cover-up and red flip-flops, and her enormous straw tote bag hangs from her elbow. It's weighing her down on one side, like she's a scale with a sandbag on one pan.

"Joseph, what are you doing back here?" Mom asks.

I want to speak, but I can't think of a single reasonable excuse for why I'd be in this part of the hotel. My mouth hangs open, and I gaze up, hoping a good reason will appear on the ceiling.

"Why does your shirt look weird?" Ben points at me.

My eyes widen when I see what he's pointing to. My tank top hangs down like I've stretched it over my head a dozen times.

Before I have a chance to answer, Mom comes in close to examine my face. "Why are you so flushed? Are you running a fever?" She places the back of her hand against my forehead.

I lean back and kind of dance away from her. I can't take all these questions. "Stop it, Ma! I'm fine!" The money in my sock scratches at my ankle. "I have to go change for the dinner shift!" I whirl around and almost run face-first into a wall.

I race down the hall like an escaped convict, and Mom's voice calls after me: "Joseph, don't run! You'll make yourself throw up again!"

I hear Ben sprinting to catch up. "Joey, wait for me!"

But I turn on my afterburners and lose him before I reach the lobby.

★ ★ ★

All evening, with every step I take, I feel the money rub against my ankle. A couple of times, the bundle shifts, and some bills slide under my foot, which is not painful but just intolerable enough to make me run back to that men's room and readjust everything. My family must think I have a serious bladder problem. Either that or they don't even notice that I'm disappearing for ten minutes at a time.

At eight o'clock, Mom finally drives my brothers and me back to my grandparents' house for the night. Every August, Bubbe insists that we stay at their house while she and Zeyde move in with Uncle Sol for the month. She says it's so my brothers and I can spread out, but I think she really just wants to keep an eye on Uncle Sol for a few weeks. Even if he's in his forties.

Ben's whining starts as soon as we get through the door. "I don't wanna take a shower! I'm not dirty! I'm too tired!" I have to admit, the kid's quite an actor. He should do Shakespeare.

Mom hugs him tight. "Sweetie, you'll just take a short one. Then you can have ice cream before you go to bed." She'll bribe him with anything to get him to give in. Ben's not having it. He throws his head back and crumples his face up. A whimpering piglet sound oozes out of him, and he jerks his whole body around, flailing his arms like a helicopter propeller. It's an impressive display, really.

Reuben sneezes from the kitchen, and Mom stomps over to him. "What's with the sneezing?" she asks. "You were sneezing the whole way here in the car. Are you getting sick?" She's alarmed and annoyed at the same time. Reuben holds his index finger up in the air and his body goes still, like he can't answer yet because he's about to discharge another sneeze. Mom doesn't wait for him to respond. She turns toward Simon, who is grabbing rolls of quarters out of a drawer. "That's the tzedakah drawer," she says. "That money is meant for charity. You can't just take it!"

"Watch me," Simon replies, and he shoves a roll of coins in each pocket. He pushes the drawer closed with his hip. "The same rolls of coins have been in that drawer since I was born. Zeyde hasn't touched them. He won't miss them."

Mom sighs in disgust, but she's got bigger fish to fry than my brother raiding the tzedakah. "You're going to sleep in the room with Ben tonight," she tells him. "Reuben's getting sick, and he should sleep by himself."

I chuckle. Sleeping with Ben is torture.

Simon skewers me with a black look. He shakes his head at Mom like this is out of the question. "There's no way I'm sleeping in a bed with Ben. It's like sleeping with a baby hippo. All he does all night is snore and fart." He glances at his watch. This is at least the third time he's done that since we left the hotel.

"He does not," Mom snaps at him.

Simon rolls his eyes. "Why do you think we call him Beans?"

Ben moves into the kitchen with the rest of us. When he hears his nickname, he puts a fist in the air and yells, "Yes!" He's quite proud of his bodily emissions.

Mom presses her fists against her hips. "Your brother is sick, Simon. Can't you think about someone else for once in your life?"

Reuben chimes in. "I'm not sick, Ma."

"See?" Simon gestures toward Reuben as if he's just given key evidence in a trial. "He's not sick!"

Mom shakes her finger in his face. "You're sleeping in Benjamin's room tonight, Simon, and that's that." She clamps her lips together.

Simon starts to move toward the laundry room. "I'm not having this conversation with you, Judy," he says. Steam comes out of Mom's ears when he calls her by her first name. He practically rips his shirt as he pulls his button-down over his head and tosses it to the floor. "I'm losing minutes of my life that I can't get back!" He grabs his Pink Floyd concert shirt and a pair of shorts from the pile of laundry on top of the dryer.

"Hold it, young man!" Mom hollers, but Simon is already pushing out the back door.

"Tick, tick, tick!" he calls out. "Away the minutes

fly!" The screen door slams, and he might as well have smacked her in the face.

"God, give me strength," Mom mutters. Her eyes are focused like lasers on the back door, and I wonder if she wants Simon to come back or not. To the three of us in the kitchen, she says, "I have a migraine. I'm going to bed." She moves toward the staircase.

"Yay!" Ben says. "I don't have to take a shower!"

Mom whirls on him. "Yes, you do! And we have to leave for New York at six in the morning, so you'd better get moving! Reuben will get you into bed." She marches up the stairs like an army officer.

"Sure, Ma, no problem," Reuben says to the air. He shuts his eyes. He looks like he could fall asleep standing up. "C'mon, Beansy. Let's go. I was supposed to call Hannah a half hour ago." Hannah is Reuben's girlfriend back in Philly. She waits by the phone for his call every night.

Reuben ushers Ben toward the stairs, and my little brother launches into "Reuben and Hannah sitting in a tree! K-I-S-S-I-N-G! First comes love . . ." I hear Reuben make a gagging sound at the top of the steps, just for effect, to make Ben laugh.

Now I'm in the kitchen alone, pressed against the wall next to the pantry. I hear the shower go on in the hallway bathroom upstairs, and Reuben and Ben chitchat away up there. Ben makes silly robot noises, and Reuben tries to settle him down so he doesn't bug Mom. I have to make a decision pretty quickly. The money in my sock needs to come out. It's sweaty and itchy and generally annoying, and now is the ideal time for me to hide it here in the house. But . . .

I really want to know where Simon's going, what it is that caused him to check his watch so much. Curiosity grips me because I never know what Simon's up to. He could just be going to meet up with a friend, but then again, who knows? He's done some boneheaded things before, like the time he shoplifted a candy bar from a gas station. I have a bad feeling that he's going to do something like that tonight. My family would be pretty impressed if I stopped him from getting in trouble, wouldn't they? They'd see the side of me that Artie saw at the arcade today. I could maybe start being Joey the Brave instead of Joey the Nervous.

I yell upstairs, "I'm going out for a walk, Reuben!" He gives no sign that he's heard me, but at least I've told the upper deck that I'm leaving the house. I race out the back door, hoping Simon hasn't gone so far already that I can't find him.

Bubbe and Zeyde's house backs up to a main road that stretches north and south as far as I can see. In the last of the day's light, it's hard to make out anything that's too far in front of me. I squint and concentrate hard as I scan the street. I don't see a soul. But I peer down the road to my right one more time . . . Is that him? I barely glimpse someone walking away from me, a blurry spot of movement, a familiar stride. That may be Simon.

I jog to catch up with him, but I sure don't want him to know I'm following him, so I keep a good two blocks' distance between us. It's definitely Simon. Now I can make out his long, skinny legs in his basketball shorts. The muggy air is so thick and still it feels like I'm running through soup.

Simon turns left at the public tennis courts, and I creep behind him as he rounds the corner toward . . . Where is he going? He's not heading for Margate's main drag with the convenience stores and pizza places. The only thing in this direction is Uncle Sol's house. Why would Simon be going there?

I've been following him for a good ten, fifteen minutes, and now the bruise color of twilight seeps into everything around me. Simon turns down Uncle Sol's street and reaches the house, but he doesn't go to the front door. What's he up to? Uncle Sol's house is dark. He and Bubbe and Zeyde are still at the hotel. Is my brother going to rob our uncle's house?

Simon hops the short picket fence surrounding the property and heads toward the backyard.

It's so quiet that I can hear my own breath coming in and out of my nose. The crickets must be worn out from the heat too, because even they sound listless tonight. Simon must have hopped the fence so he wouldn't have to open the creaky gate and risk alerting the neighbors. Now I have to decide whether to do the same thing.

As I stand there gripping the gate lock, the bass beat of a car radio pounds through the air. A car pulls up to the curb a half block away. The driver kills the engine but doesn't exit the car. The hair on the back of my neck stands up. I'd better make a move. I'm not sure I can make it over the fence, so I unlatch the gate and swing it open. It doesn't make a sound. I let out a grunt of relief. Someone must have oiled the hinges recently.

I hug the side of the house and steal toward the back-yard. Simon's nowhere to be seen. I jump when I hear some muffled noises coming from the shed at the back of the yard. Weak light leaks under the shed's door. I see a figure move across the yard from the opposite side of the house. The squishy patter of flip-flops accompanies a head of white hair coming across the lawn. The figure raps at the shed door. The door swings open, and the blonde squeals and starts giggling. A girl! Simon wraps his arm around her waist and pulls her into the shed. He glances left and right, scanning the backyard. Then he disappears into the shed again and shuts the door.

Huh. I plunk myself onto the grass behind a tree. This makes no sense to me. If Simon is meeting up with a girl, why do it at Uncle Sol's shed? Is this girl on the lam or something?

After a while, the odor of cigarettes cuts the night air, stinging the hair in my nose. I lean over and look around the tree toward the shed. Soft laughter and the faint trill of a transistor radio float toward me across the lawn.

Uncle Sol would have a stroke if he knew about this. I rub my eyes so hard it hurts. I should just go back to Bubbe and Zeyde's place and go to sleep. I probably wasn't going to confront Simon anyway, no matter what he was doing. Has one afternoon in an arcade convinced me I'm some kind of hotshot now? Like I'd be able to stop Simon from doing anything?

The cigarette smell hits the back of my throat, and I start coughing. *Oh, man, that was loud!* The radio snaps off, as do the whispers and giggles. The door to the shed swings open, and Simon's voice comes at me like a slap. "Joey!" I try to stifle my cough, but it's obviously too late to pretend I'm not here. He barks my name again.

"Yeah?" I cringe and bite down on my lip.

Simon pounces at me through the darkness. Something between a gurgle and a squeal spurts out of me.

"What are you doing? You followed me here?" He grabs my arm and pulls me toward the shed.

Well, obviously, I think, but I keep my mouth shut. Anything I say will make him angrier. That "hero" feeling I had a few minutes ago? Totally gone now.

We reach the doorway. Simon has pushed all of Uncle Sol's stuff against the walls of the shed and put a small folding table and two folding chairs right in the middle of the tiny space. The light inside comes from a huge flashlight sitting on the table, shining up at the ceiling. Threads of nauseating smoke spiral into the air from a cigarette in an ashtray next to the flashlight. The girl I saw earlier is balancing on the back legs of a folding chair. When she sees me, she slams the front legs onto the concrete floor and laughs. "Who's this?" she asks Simon.

I'm his brother! Who are you?

Simon picks up the ashtray and crushes the end of the cigarette against it. He's glaring at me. I'm pretty sure he's conjuring up methods of torture for me. "He's my brother."

The girl stands up and smiles at me like I'm a kitten in a pet store window. Even in the dull light I can see that she's a slim blonde with vivid blue eyes. "You didn't tell me you have a little brother!"

Simon places the ashtray on the table. "This is Joey."

The girl offers me her hand to shake, which I take because if I don't, I won't know what to do with myself.

"Well, hi, Joey. I'm Farrah." Her smile is kind of dazzling, and I guess I'm staring at her like she's a swimsuit model because Simon spins me around and points me back toward the yard.

"Okay, bye, Joey." He pushes me forward so hard I almost end up on my knees in the grass.

"It's okay, Si," Farrah says. I turn around to see her plant a kiss on his cheek. "I have to go anyway."

"You just got here!" Is he using a baby voice? I've never, ever heard Simon sound like that. He puts his arms around her waist and kisses her twice on the lips. I should probably let someone know that my brother has been replaced by an alien.

"I'm sorry," Farrah murmurs, peeling Simon's hands off of her. "But my dad will be home any minute, and if I'm not there, he'll flip. You know how he feels about you." She starts across the backyard, then spins and wiggles her fingers at me. "Bye, Joey! Nice to meet you!" And she bounds off into the darkness.

Simon folds up the little table and chairs, places them against the back wall, and moves some of the random junk in the shed back to the middle of the space. He won't look at me.

I'm shifting from foot to foot on the grass outside the shed. I can't stand his silence. "She seems nice." I roll my eyes at myself. *Brilliant comment, Joey.*

"Zip it, squirt." Simon switches off the flashlight, places it in a corner, and comes out of the shed. He closes the door and locks it with a combination lock he lifts out of the grass. "You had no business following me here and"—he throws his hands up—"interrupting like that." He passes by me, and I have to hurry to catch up to him so I don't lose him in the dark.

"Is she your girlfriend?"

He rounds on me and leans in close. The cigarette smell clings to him. "Are you serious?" He darts his head around, like he's making sure our parents aren't nearby. "Does she look Jewish to you?"

Now I get it. Simon has to meet with her someplace private so my family doesn't find out he's seeing a girl who's not Jewish. Uncle Sol never goes in that shed. I'd even bet the stuff in there belongs to the previous owner of his house. They're hiding in plain sight.

"What did she mean when she said you know how her father feels about you?"

Simon looks at me like he can't believe he has to explain this to me. "What do you think?"

I drop my eyes to the ground. "Oh." Her dad doesn't want her dating a Jew any more than my parents want Simon dating a gentile. So Simon and I have something in common now: we're both hiding things from our family, and neither one of us is too happy about it.

Simon grabs my chin and squeezes my face hard. "If you say anything to anyone about her, if I even think you're thinking about her, you'll regret it. Understand?"

I nod.

He lets me go and storms off without looking back. Before I take a single step toward home, I watch his back until he disappears into the darkness. I think leaving some distance between us isn't such a bad idea.

★ ★ ★

Simon is stomping up the stairs when I walk in the back door of the house. He stops halfway and groans. He's probably just remembered that he's supposed to sleep with Ben tonight. I wait until I hear a door creak open and closed. I have one last thing to do before I crawl up to bed.

I can't get my sneakers off fast enough. The wad of bills is stuck to my foot like Saran wrap, damp and wrinkly, and I peel it off. I shuffle through drawers in the kitchen looking for an envelope to stuff the money into, but I can't find one.

Bubbe always keeps a stack of old mail and newspapers in the laundry room—for what purpose, I don't know—but I find an ancient electric bill in a yellowed envelope in the middle of the pile. I check the bill. It's from 1972. I assume this has been paid by now. I shove the bill back into the pile and take the envelope.

The money fits in it, barely. I dart through the house on the way to the hiding place I've been thinking about all day. In the formal living room where no one ever sits, my extended family watches me from a wall of framed photographs. I don't recognize most of the faces in the black-and-white photos, but Bubbe has taught me everyone's name and how we're related: great-great-aunts and -uncles and long-dead cousins from the Broder side of the family. A few Goodman pictures hang together on one side of the wall—a photo of my parents and my brothers and me from Reuben's bar mitzvah four years ago, one of all of us sitting around the seder table, and one where Ben is lighting the Chanukah candles. Everyone stares down at me. They know what I'm up to. *Hiding gambling money from the family is not something nice Jewish boys do, Joey.*

I head for the storage room. Years ago, Bubbe and Zeyde converted the garage into an extra room, and they connected it to the rest of the house through big double doors in the dining room. The storage room is filled with all kinds of junk—stacks of old St. Bonaventure dishes and bowls, beat-up plastic toys from when my brothers and I were little, shelves of ancient books. You name it, it's in the storage room. And the only reason anyone goes in there now is because there's a freezer chest in the room that Bubbe keeps stocked with ice cream bars.

I step inside the storage room and feel around for the light switch on the wall to my right. When I flip the switch, two bare bulbs glint in the darkness. I make my way across the cluttered floor. It's like going through a field of land mines. I can barely find clear spots to place my feet. A spider skitters across my path, drawing my eyes to a pile of paperback books that have probably been sitting there since the 1950s. I take the first two books off the pile and place the envelope of money on top of the third book. Then I put the other two books back on top. I bend and stoop, checking out the pile from different angles. Pressed between the books, the envelope is completely hidden, snug as a bug in a rug. "Perfect," I whisper.

I make my way back the way I came in, flicking off the light and shutting the door. Now my exhaustion really hits me. My eyes burn for sleep. I trudge up the stairs, and I don't even brush my teeth before I slump onto my foldaway cot in the fourth bedroom.

I can still feel the deep imprint that the roll of cash made against my ankle. Simon's threats sit like a weight in my stomach, but at least I'm absolutely sure no one's going to find my money.

CHAPTER 4

By Saturday morning, I'm crawling out of my skin. I can't stop thinking about going to Pinky's later and talking to Artie Bishop about *The Once and Future King*. I'll be impressed if he's read the whole book in two days because it's like six hundred pages long. But I'll bet he did. I'll bet he has all kinds of ideas he wants to talk about.

My plan for getting out of working the lunch shift today forms in my head. It involves a little deception, which I feel bad about but not that bad. I have to get out of here, and I'm not going to let a waiter-in-training shift stop me. As Reuben and I set the tables for lunch, I slump into a chair.

"You okay, squirt?" Reuben asks. He folds a cloth napkin into a fan and places it on a plate.

I sigh. "Yeah, I'm fine. Just have a headache. I'll be okay." I rub my eyes with the heels of my palms and slowly push myself up to stand. I could give Ben a run for his money with this performance.

I glance at the clock on the far wall. If I show up at

Pinky's at noon exactly, won't that make me seem overly eager? But if I get there too late, I may insult Artie, and it seems like those guys are easily insulted. The sweet spot, I figure, is 12:10, about forty minutes from now.

My act continues. I lean against a waiter's station and drop my head to my chest. I close my eyes and breathe heavily. Minutes slide by, and no one notices me. I'm starting to get a little aggravated about that, but I have to be disciplined. Keep this up.

Finally, Reuben comes over and hands me a glass of water. "Bad headache, huh?"

I take a small sip, like that's all I can manage. "I think I'm going to go take some aspirin and lie down."

Reuben feels my forehead. "You don't feel warm, so that's good. Where are you going to go?" His concern is so sincere that I almost can't go through with this. Almost.

"I'll just grab a room key and go into a vacant room," I say. "Is that okay? I'm sorry."

"It's no problem, squirt. Go lie down. No one will bother you."

"Okay, thanks. I'm sure I'll be fine in a little while. Can you tell Bubbe for me?" Bubbe's like the military police: she knows things without anyone knowing how she knows them. She would see through this scheme in seconds. I can't risk actually speaking to her.

"Sure," Reuben says. A twinge of guilt stabs me in the side. I didn't mean to get Reuben involved in my lie.

But what matters is that I'm out the dining room door, walking toward the lobby. All I need to do is grab a room key from behind the front desk, go make the room look like I've been lying on the bed in case anyone comes looking for me, and sneak out onto the Boardwalk.

I pull open the drawer where the room keys are kept . . . and draw back in alarm. Why are there so many keys in the drawer? Why are there so many rooms available? It's August, and the St. Bonaventure is only half full. A Boardwalk hotel shouldn't be half full at the height of summer. No wonder Uncle Sol is sighing so much lately. Why isn't anyone doing anything about this? We should put an ad in the paper or lower the room prices or something, shouldn't we?

My stomach drops as my eyes sweep across the lobby. The ceramic frogs around the fountain gurgle up water. The sound is so familiar to me, like my mother's voice. An old lady sits in one of the high-back leather chairs, reading the newspaper. When Ben and I were little, we used to curl up and fall asleep on those chairs.

I don't know what would happen to my family without this hotel. I don't know who we'd be without it.

"What are you doing back here, Joey?" George, the bell captain, appears beside me.

I blink at him. What will happen to George if the St. Bonaventure goes under? Or Lionel, the elevator operator, or all the people who work in the kitchen, or—

"What's the matter, kiddo?"

I have to look away. "Oh, nothing. I just have a headache. I was going to go lie down in one of the empty rooms."

George takes the key to Room 218 from the drawer and hands it to me. "Go on. You look like you could use some peace and quiet. Not much of that in this place."

The gold *218* is mostly rubbed off of the green plastic of the key holder. Uncle Sol should have replaced these years ago. I rub my thumb over what's left of the number. "George, is the hotel in trouble?"

He squeezes my shoulder. His hand is strong and calloused. His eyes are gentle. "Who can say, Joey? Gambling's going to be legal in Atlantic City soon. The casinos are going to take over the Boardwalk. I know that much. But that's not something you should be worrying about. You'll always have the St. Bonaventure in one form or another, even if it's only in your heart."

My head hangs down. That's not part of today's act. "Thanks, George," I squeeze out, and I mope toward the elevator.

Up in Room 218, I sit down on the edge of the bed. I wonder what the future holds for my grandparents.

Uncle Sol can go work at another hotel, maybe even a casino hotel, if gambling comes to Atlantic City like everyone says it will. But it won't be this hotel, our hotel.

Before I let my imagination go too far down that hole, I sidle over to the bathroom sink and splash cool water on my face. I have to get out of here. It's quarter to twelve already, and I have places to be. Well, one place to be. That little twist of excitement in my stomach returns.

Getting out of the hotel isn't as tough as I thought it might be. I take the service elevator down to the laundry room level. Then I creep along the cinder block walls until I reach a little-used side entrance to the hotel. I've been exploring the St. Bonaventure for enough years to know the ins and outs that no one thinks I know.

In a flash, I'm outside, next to two big dumpsters in the side parking lot where the employees park their old Chevys and Datsuns. A ramp about a block away leads up onto the Boardwalk, past where my family's eyes will roam if anyone is looking out a window on this side of the hotel. My heartbeat picks up speed.

The breeze on the Boardwalk comes at me in muggy gusts. The sun is somewhere up there struggling to burn through the thick, humid cloud cover. Rolling chairs *tick-tick-tick* across the boards as they flow around me and pass by, the passengers *ooo*-ing and *ahh*-ing on their scenic tours. I stick close to the storefronts, hugging the half-hearted shade from their awnings and catching an aggressive blast of air-conditioning when someone opens a door as I walk by.

I didn't have a chance to change my clothes, so I'm still wearing my waiter's duds: white button-down shirt, khaki pants, and synagogue shoes. But maybe this is better than showing up at Pinky's in shorts, a hand-me-down T-shirt, and trashed sneakers, right? As usual, my mind starts spinning, kicking the rock down the road until I lose it in the gravel. I'm on my way to a bar to meet a guy I hardly know who surrounds himself with questionable friends. What does he want from a thirteen-year-old Skee-Ball-playing nobody, anyway? Is he going to force me to play Skee-Ball for the rest of the afternoon so he can win some money? My family's going to miss me at some point, aren't they? I'm halfway there before I realize I haven't thought this through at all.

But my feet continue moving me forward until Pinky's silver door handle is in my grip. I hesitate, but a guy behind me says, "You going in or what, kid?" I do want to go in. If nothing else, I want to get my book back. So, in I go.

They really need to fix the AC in here. I thought it was hot on the Boardwalk. This is worse because your hopes are up that it'll be cool inside.

I reach the half-wall that separates the arcade from the bar and restaurant. I've been in a bar before. The St. Bonaventure has a bar just off the dining room. The bartender's name is Oscar, and he slipped me a shot of whisky last summer that made me feel like my teeth were melting. Just the smell of liquor sickens me, so I'm not surprised when my stomach starts to churn.

Some people sit around tables, and two drunks at the end of the bar growl at each other. Ralphie's voice rings out over the sound of the TV: "Good-man!" I find him with Artie at a table across the room. Sweat trickles down my back as I approach them.

But Ralphie is all smiles. "Good-man! How are you today?" He nods at an empty chair. "Have a seat." His huge mitts make his glass of beer look like it belongs in a dollhouse. Artie swirls something amber-colored with lots of ice in his glass.

I pull out the chair and lower myself down like they might have put a thumbtack on the seat. Artie leans back in his chair and clasps his hands in front of him. He's not wearing a tie today, just a light blue button-down shirt with the sleeves rolled up to his elbows, and brown slacks. "Hello, Joey," he says, calm as a purring cat.

"Hi." I somehow accomplish a smile. I don't know what to do with my hands, so I grip the seat of the chair like I'm trying to keep myself from floating away.

Artie smiles without showing his teeth. It's a cool smile. He's not sure about me yet. That's okay. I'm not sure about him either. He snaps his fingers in the air to get the bartender's attention. "Hey, Tommy, can we get this kid a Coke?" He turns back to me. "Joey, how's your day going so far?"

"It's fine." I thought I came here to discuss *The Once and Future King* and get my book back. I don't even see the book. It's not on the table or in his hands or anywhere.

Artie tilts his head to the side. "You look like you're about to wet yourself, kid. What are you afraid of?"

Well, that list is pretty long. "Nothing. I'm not afraid." And I shrug, trying to look casual.

"Good." Artie nods. "You're dressed up. You going somewhere special today?"

"No, I was just working. I'm a waiter. I have to dress like this for work."

Artie and Ralphie glance at each other. How could that have been the wrong thing to say?

"Where do you wait tables?" Artie asks.

"At the St. Bonaventure."

Ralphie points at my head. "So that's why you're wearing the little beanie. Ain't that a hotel for Jewish types?"

My kippah! How could I forget to take it off? "Yeah,

it's a kosher hotel," I say. I yank the kippah from my head and tuck it away in my pocket.

Ralphie chimes in. "We figured you was a Jew anyway, kid. I mean, look at you. You sure ain't Irish." He chortles and wipes at the folds of his neck with a napkin.

I stare at the tabletop.

"Shut up, Ralphie," Artie snaps at him. "You talk too much." He scoots his chair forward. "So, Joey, you came here to talk about your book."

The bartender brings over a glass of soda, and I gulp half of it down without coming up for air.

"Tell me what you like about that book so much," Artie says.

"Well, I guess I like that Wart is just this nobody kid at the beginning, but then he becomes the king."

Artie nods. "He becomes a legendary king. King Arthur."

Ralphie chuckles. "King Arthur? That's like you, Artie! You're King Artie!" He grabs my shoulder and shakes me a little. "Get it, kid? He's the king around here. He's the king of Steel Pier. Right, Artie?" He raises his beer. "To King Artie! The king of Steel Pier!" He chugs. "Hey, Tommy!" he yells toward the bar. "Tommy, where's our food already? The king of Steel Pier wants his burger!"

hotel pretty soon. Mom-and-pop hotels aren't going to survive on the Boardwalk once the casinos come."

"Everyone keeps saying that," I mutter. My mind jumps back to all of those room keys I saw earlier.

"They'll make a ton of dough, though, when they sell."

How do I explain to him that money isn't the important thing here? That I care about the frogs in the lobby fountain and Shabbat dinner and fixing leaky faucets with Zeyde. I want to keep talking to Artie, but I don't want to talk about this.

Artie must know that because he changes the subject real quick. "How old are you, Joey? Thirteen? Fourteen?"

"Thirteen." I force myself to straighten up again.

"You get good grades in school?"

I shrug. "Pretty good." That's my dad's usual response when he sees my report card full of Bs. I do get As in math, so he's happy about that.

"Are you making good money at your waiter job?"

"I'm not making any money. I'm a waiter-in-training."

"Would you like to make some real money?"

"Um . . ."

Artie smiles at me. "Of course you would. So, I think I may have a job for you. If you're interested."

I clutch my hands together on my lap. "What kind of job?"

"Well, on Monday, my daughter, my little girl, is

coming to visit me for a couple of weeks. She lives with her mom, you understand, so I don't get to see her all the time. But she's coming to Atlantic City for two weeks. Now, I want to spend as much time with her as I can, but she can't be with me all day while I'm working, right? You don't go to work with your dad all day, right? So I'm looking for someone to be her—how can I put this—her chaperone, her companion, while she's here. You know, a couple of hours a day, take her on the rides at one of the piers, teach her how to play Skee-Ball, maybe go to the beach. And then bring her back here in the afternoon when I'm done with work for the day. Does that sound like a job you might be interested in?"

So he wants a babysitter for his daughter. I baby-sit for Ben all the time when Mom and Dad go out on the weekends, and they don't pay me a dime. I've never babysat for a girl, but how hard can it be?

I don't say anything for a few seconds, not because I'm going to say no but because my mind is already trying to work out how I can say yes and still wait tables with my brothers at the hotel.

Artie senses my hesitation. "You probably want to know what kind of money we're talking about here, right? I mean, you don't want to do it if it's not worth your while, I'm sure."

"Well . . ."

"I like you, Joey. I think you're a very responsible and trustworthy boy. I'm right about that, aren't I?"

I crush the fingers of my right hand with my left. He doesn't know that I've lied to my entire family just to be in this room with him. "Uh-huh."

"And I wouldn't trust my little girl with just anybody. But I have a feeling about you. I think you're perfect for this job. I think I can trust you, and I think you're going to be a great chaperone." He points both of his index fingers at me and nods, like we have an understanding.

"I don't know. I have a commitment to the hotel, and—"

"Twenty-five bucks a week," he says. "For two weeks. So, fifty bucks. You take care of my girl from ten to four. On the weekdays only, mind you, not the weekends. And I'll pay you fifty bucks. How does that sound? Are you in?"

Considering my current salary is zero bucks a week, the offer is excellent. *Should I do this?* Under the table, my foot's tapping a mile a minute.

My lag in answering must make Artie think I'm some kind of ace negotiator because he says, "All right, thirty bucks a week, so sixty bucks total. You drive a hard bargain, kid."

I can't help but smile. I think I just out-negotiated

the—what did Ralphie call him?—the king of Steel Pier! The king of Steel Pier is going to pay me sixty bucks!

We shake hands, and Artie pats my shoulder. "You're one of the guys now, Joey!"

For exactly six seconds, I'm thrilled. After those six seconds, I feel a real headache coming on.

CHAPTER 5

As I walk back to the hotel, my mind fills with menacing thoughts about how this is all going to go wrong. I don't know what it is about Artie Bishop that makes me want to please him, but I do. He's the total opposite of my father. Artie wouldn't shake his head at me and make me leave the room. No, Artie talks to me like I'm an adult, like I'm his equal. He's interested in what I have to say. If I can just figure out how I'm going to pull this off, this babysitting thing, I'm in the clear. I can't keep claiming to be sick every day I'm supposed to work the lunch shift.

I reach the St. Bonaventure and push through the revolving door. What I need is some brilliant idea about how to convince Bubbe that I—

"Joey!"

Uncle Sol stands directly in front of me, arms crossed over his wide chest, like he's in the Secret Service.

"Oh, hey, Uncle Sol," I croak. Uncle Sol is a big guy. He blocks my whole field of vision. I picture him picking me up by the scruff of my neck, like I'm a stray kitten, and depositing me at Bubbe's feet.

"What were you doing on the Boardwalk, young man? I heard you were sleeping off a terrible headache."

I close my eyes, like my response is written on the back of my eyelids. All I can come up with is, "I just went outside for some air."

Uncle Sol considers me for a moment. I focus on a mystery stain on the burgundy carpet.

Finally, Uncle Sol says, "You don't look so good. You should go lie down." He walks away, humming, just like Zeyde does.

Go lie down, Joey. This is how they all see me, as the kid who needs to lie down. I stand there for a long time, fuming. I'm thirteen. According to Jewish law, that means I'm a man. I've known Artie less than a week, and he already sees that I'm tough. I've known my family my whole life, and they still think I'm the weakling. Maybe that's what I'll always be to them.

Artie called me "one of the guys." That sure sounds strong to me.

* * *

It's Sunday, the day before my babysitting job starts. Mom and Bubbe are buzzing around the kitchen at my grandparents' house, getting brunch ready. Days when we're all together and other employees run the hotel don't happen that often, maybe once or twice in the whole month of August. We all squeeze around the dining room table, and Bubbe and Mom bring out tons of food. Dishes and platters smother the white vinyl tablecloth.

Finally, Mom and Bubbe sit down. That means we can all attack the platters in front of us. "There's enough food here to feed an army!" Uncle Sol says, but we always manage to polish most of it off.

When he's finished eating, Ben burps loudly and announces, "I'm done!"

Together, Reuben and Simon yell, "Beans!" Ben laughs and leaves the table.

Uncle Sol spoons some tuna salad onto his plate. "Reuben, it's time to start thinking about college."

Dad rolls his eyes. Like he and Reuben haven't spoken about college before.

Reuben says, "I've got it figured out, Uncle Sol. I'm going to apply to Penn State."

Uncle Sol nods. "That's an excellent school. Plenty of Jewish kids there too."

Mom pats her mouth with her napkin. "I don't want him to go so far away."

"It's not that far, Ma," Reuben says.

Simon shovels a slice of tomato into his mouth. "I'm going to go to college in California."

"No, you're not," Mom says. "And don't talk with your mouth full."

Simon chomps on his tomato and makes exaggerated chewing sounds.

"How far is Penn State from our house?" I ask Reuben.

"It's around a three, three-and-a-half-hour drive," he says.

I take a long, slow bite of my bagel. "That's pretty far."

"You can come visit me, squirt."

"Can I, Dad?"

"Can you what?" Dad replies without looking up from his plate.

"Can I visit Reuben at Penn State?"

Dad sips his coffee. "We'll see."

When parents say "We'll see," it's their way of spending as little time thinking about what you've asked them as they can.

A few minutes later, when Mom and Bubbe have gone to the kitchen to start washing the dishes, Ben bursts out of the storage room holding something over his head. "I'm rich! I'm rich!" He scoots around the table to stand next to Reuben. "Look what I found!" He thrusts his arms out so everyone can see. He's holding an old, yellowed envelope stuffed with money.

Ben found my money.

I choke on the last bite of my poppy seed bagel.

Reuben takes the envelope from him. "Where'd you find this, Beans?"

Ben waves his arm toward the storage room. "I wanted a Nutty Buddy, so I went to get one from the freezer. And then I saw this pile of books, and on top was the book *Jaws*—you know, like the movie. So I went to get the book, but I kind of tripped and knocked over the books, and the envelope must've been just sitting there in the pile!"

Ben explains all of this while Reuben counts the money. A huge knot blocks my throat, and it's not the bagel.

"Wow, Beans," Reuben says. "This is a lot of money. You have to tell Bubbe. It must be her money."

"But I found it!" Ben's face crunches up. "Finders keepers!"

My whole head gets hot. My vision blurs. What am I supposed to do now?

"Ma! Bubbe! Beans found a pile of money in the storage room!" Simon yells.

My mother and grandmother hustle into the dining room from the kitchen. Bubbe wipes her wet hands on her apron, and Reuben hands her the envelope. Ben presses his palms together under his chin. "Bubbe, can't I have it? Please, please, please? I found it!"

We're all quiet while Bubbe inspects the envelope, her face pinched. "Where did you find this, bubbeleh?"

"In the storage room. In a pile of books."

I wipe at my eyes with the back of my hands.

"A pile of books? In my storage room?" Bubbe sounds confused.

Yes, a pile of paperbacks that no one ever looks at. The place no one would ever think to look.

Bubbe shakes her head. "I must have put it in there so long ago, I don't even remember it."

Or maybe Joey earned it when he won a bunch of money for some shady guys at the arcade he shouldn't even have been in. Yeah, maybe that.

Bubbe hands the envelope back to Ben. "Take the money, Benjamin. Split it with your brothers." My lunch comes back up a little.

Ben whoops. "But I get to keep most of it, right, Bubbe? 'Cause I found it?"

Simon rolls his eyes. "What do you need money for, Beans? You don't buy anything. Besides, you make a ton of money on those commercials."

Ben snorts at Simon. "Mom says that money's for college, dummy."

Everyone starts talking at once. All I hear is *keep, money, yours, mine, no, please, money, money!*

Reuben's voice rises above the rest. "We're going to

split it! It's thirty-two bucks each." He starts making four small piles.

Simon pushes the knife in a little further. "Somebody only gets thirty-one. Give Joey thirty-one."

I can't take it anymore. I push my chair back and bolt to the bathroom near the back door. I lean over the sink and stare at the swirling pattern of the porcelain. This was not supposed to happen. No one was supposed to find that money. Will there ever be a time when I don't feel like I'm sunken in a hole and everyone is just stepping over me? God could have helped me out here, right? But no. I'm the afterthought of my family, and I'm an afterthought for God too. Not that I even believe He's up there. Not that I even care.

I stare at my reflection in the mirror above the sink. *Wait.* I was offered a job yesterday. I was offered a job by Artie Bishop, the king of Steel Pier. He wants me to babysit his daughter. He picked me. He said I'm one of the guys now. That means something.

I splash my face and neck with cold water. I feel every droplet cover my skin, like I'm putting on a mask. I go back to the dining room, sit down, and count my short stack of bills like I don't care at all.

★ ★ ★

Later, Dad leaves to drive back to our house in Philly for the week. Everyone left at Bubbe and Zeyde's place is tired and cranky, and we sit silently in the living room, staring at the television, for the next hour. The show is about animals of the Serengeti. I gape at the screen until the final credits come on and Mom snaps off the TV. "Let's go. Everyone up to bed. You're a bunch of zombies sitting here."

"But it's only eight o'clock," Ben whines.

"Benjamin, if you last until eight thirty I'll be stunned," she replies. "Now go."

Uncle Sol drives Bubbe and Zeyde back to his house for the night. When I watch my grandparents vacate their own home, I feel like an intruder. No one else seems to mind.

I flop down on my cot. Tomorrow's a big day for me, so I'll need a good night's sleep. I clench my covers and listen to my stomach making all kinds of weird noises. Mom would tell me it's just gas—she says that everything that bothers one of us in the stomach area is gas. I'm nervous, all right. But Artie thinks I'm going to make a great chaperone. He thinks I'm special. That's more than I can say for the people around here.

CHAPTER 6

On the drive to the hotel on Monday morning, Ben chatters away, as usual, and every few minutes my mom says "Uh-huh" like she's really paying attention. It's fine with me, though, because I don't have to talk to anyone. I'm not working the lunch shift today, so I don't need to think up any excuses for Bubbe. And I don't need Uncle Sol's money, so I don't have to play that ridiculous game with him. At quarter of ten, I troop down the Boardwalk toward Pinky's to meet up with my boss, Artie Bishop.

I'm walking to work, to my new job.

I straighten my spine and lift my chin. Artie has given me a lot to think about in the last week or so—about how important it is to be strong and have faith in myself. I never talk to my dad or Reuben or even Zeyde about stuff like that. I hope I get to spend more time with Artie now that I'll be working for him. If I do a good job at this babysitting gig, Artie might take me right under his wing. My stomach flutters a little just thinking about that possibility.

I reach the door with the big silver handle. It's only my third time entering Pinky's, but I already feel like I'm opening the door to someplace I belong. Inside, everything's as I left it on Saturday. The AC buzzes like an old man snoring, and the ceiling fans in the bar area spread around a haze of cigarette smoke. A bearded man at the bar calls out "Good-man!" and I raise a hand in greeting. I don't see Artie, but Ralphie and Grunts are deep in conversation at one of the tables, their heads tilted toward each other.

I hear Ralphie mutter, "Soon, Grunts, soon. We'll make our move, and he'll never see it coming." Ralphie bangs his fist on the tabletop when he says the word *never*. Grunts nods and digs his cigarette into an ashtray like he's smashing someone's face into the ground. What are they talking about? *Who* will never see *what* coming?

I startle a bit when they whip their heads up at me. Ralphie shouts, "Joey the Good-man! How you doin' today?" He reaches out and pumps my arm like he's going to get water out of me. "Have a seat, kid. Artie'll be here any minute with Melanie."

I sit on the edge of a chair at their table and watch Ralphie slurp from his cup of coffee. Grunts tries to smile at me, but it looks more like a fishhook is pulling at the corner of his upper lip. I nod to him and look away. I cannot maintain eye contact with that man.

The minutes go by. I start tapping my feet and moving my eyes over the wood beams of the ceiling. Something about the snippet of conversation I just overheard scratches at my skull, and I shudder.

The back door opens, and in steps Artie, wearing his tan suit and his red tie. He's backlit from the sunlight coming in through the doorway, and it's like he's surrounded by fire. His thick dark hair is combed back, and he looks as cool as Clint Eastwood in *Dirty Harry*. Everyone in the place stops what they're doing to say hello to him. But as soon as he sees me, he comes right over with a big grin. "Joey!" he says, and he shakes my hand. "How are you today? You ready for your new job?"

"Sure," I reply, and I lean into my grip on his hand.

"Great, great. First, we need to set some ground rules here. Rule number one is you don't take your eyes off my little girl, understand?"

"Yes, sir."

Artie swings his head toward Ralphie and Grunts. "Did you hear that? He just called me 'sir.' I like that. Why don't you two knuckleheads call me 'sir'?" Ralphie chuckles. Grunts gives his fishhook smile again. "Rule number two is go easy on the junk food. I don't need you bringing my girl back to me all sloppy and sick." I nod. "And rule number three, Joey? Keep her away from the boys, and keep the boys away from her. She can hang around with you, but no other boys, got it?"

No other boys? Before I can ask Artie what he's talking about, someone comes in through the back door.

Oh.

The someone is a girl, all right, but I realize immediately that I am in a ton of trouble. This girl, who must be Melanie because she greets Ralphie and Grunts and the other people around her like she's known them all her life, is not a little girl. She's a teenager. She's got to be fifteen! Her hair is long and straight and black as ink, and she's a few inches taller than me. She's wearing a yellow tank top with a big, red Hawaiian flower on it, and white cut-off shorts. I've never seen a person so beautiful in my life.

Artie takes her by the arm and leads her over to me. "Mel, this is Joey Goodman, the kid I told you about. Joey, this is my daughter, Melanie."

She reaches her hand out, and I know I'm supposed to shake it, but I just stand there staring. Her eyes are light brown—hazel, really—and she has a dimple on her right cheek when she smiles. She takes my hand and places it in hers and starts shaking them together. "Hello, Joey Goodman," she says.

All I can grunt out is "Hi."

Artie puts a hand on each of our shoulders. "I expect you back by four o'clock. Not four-oh-one. Four.

Understand? Or else I'm going to send people out to find you, and nobody wants that, right?"

Melanie kisses Artie on the cheek. "Sure thing, Pops."

Artie presses a short stack of dollar bills into my hand. "That's ten bucks. I expect change, Joey. Now go have fun. And be back by four."

Melanie grabs my wrist and pulls me away from her father and his men. "Come on, kid," she says to me over her shoulder. "Let's get this show on the road!"

Things have taken an unexpected turn. Melanie and her soft, soft hand lead me out onto the Boardwalk, and I smile like I've just won the lottery.

* * *

"Okay, Joey Goodman, what do you have on our schedule for today?" The hot breeze thrashes Melanie's hair around until she pulls an elastic band out of her pocket and gathers it all into a ponytail. She's even prettier with her hair back because now I can see her whole face from ear to ear. She has a very cute little birthmark on her left cheek that's shaped like an amoeba. She snaps her fingers in front of my face. "Hello? Earth to Goodman? Do you speak?"

"Oh, yeah, sorry." I strike what I hope is a cool, casual pose.

Melanie puts her fingers into her belt loops and shifts her hip over to one side. "So, you're my shadow for the next two weeks."

"I guess so." I shrug, like this isn't ideal for me either.

She looks me over for a minute. "I hope you can keep up with me. You don't want to end up like last year's choice."

"What do you mean? I'm not the first one to do this? To be your . . . chaperone?"

Melanie lets out a deep, husky laugh that makes my stomach flutter. "Is that what my dad is calling it this year? No, there's always someone assigned to me while I'm here. Last year it was Eddie, if you can believe that."

"Eddie? Really?"

She laughs again. "He lost me an hour into the first day! I wasn't even trying to shake him! He was out of breath a hundred feet down the Boardwalk!"

We start walking south, away from Pinky's, away from the St. Bonaventure. Melanie is wearing yellow flip-flops, and her toenails are painted bright pink. "How old are you, Joey Goodman?"

Should I lie and tell her I'm fifteen? Would she even believe me? I wouldn't believe me. "I'm thirteen, but I'll be fourteen soon." If you consider next March soon. "How old are you?"

"Fifteen. Sixteen in a couple of months."

"One of my brothers is sixteen."

"One of your brothers? You have more than one?"

"I have three. Ben is ten, Simon is sixteen, and Reuben is seventeen. You have any brothers or sisters?"

Melanie presses her lips together. "Uh, no. Just me." She looks down at her feet as we walk. "So, you want to go to Million Dollar Pier, or what? I've been looking forward to winning a huge stuffed animal all summer."

Million Dollar Pier is like Steel Pier's kid brother: smaller but more entertaining. Still, at ten o'clock on a Monday morning, it doesn't exactly bustle with activity. I guess parents have taken their kids to the beach. Melanie and I stand at the entrance, taking it in for a minute.

"There's nobody here," she says, shading her eyes with her hand. "Isn't this supposed to be the fun pier?"

"It's still pretty early. Maybe it will get crowded this afternoon."

"By then we'll have won all the prizes!" She takes me by the elbow and starts toward the midway. Her hand is smooth and warm on my skin.

About forty feet ahead of us sits a flat-roofed, rectangular building around the size of a two-car garage, made of worn wood slats. Huge bullhorn speakers on the roof's corners blast a man's voice on a loop: "Come see the ape woman! Watch her transform before your eyes from woman to ape!"

This announcement and that building have always scared the daylights out of me. Last summer, I stood outside by myself while Reuben and Simon went in to see the show. Afterward, Simon called me a baby, and I didn't even care. As long as I didn't have to be inside that building.

Behind the voice on the bullhorns come the howls and calls of hyenas and monkeys and elephants, as well as the endless beating of drums. I guess it's all to lure people in. I know it's probably just a silly circus-type show, but you still couldn't pay me to go in there.

"Want to see the ape woman?" Melanie asks. She scrunches her mouth over to the left side of her face, which I assume is her skeptical face.

"No, definitely not," I reply, and I walk around the building to the left and onto the main part of the midway. Melanie is right behind me.

"What's wrong? You scared?" She's trying to taunt me, but I keep my eyes straight ahead.

"It's a waste of money," I say with a shrug. "She doesn't really turn into an ape, you know. It's just a show."

"No kidding." She rolls her eyes. "But it's got to be hilarious! What do you think they do, flash the lights a bunch of times and put her in an ape suit?"

My idea of the "transformation" has always been vague, but it never fails to make me queasy. "Who knows?"

"Well, I still want to see it. It'll be a riot!"

No, it won't. Creepy and terrifying, more likely.

I silently thank God when Melanie is distracted by the midway games, and we go up to the first booth. She leans over the wood counter in front of us, trying to figure out the game.

"Three tries for a quarter," the bored-looking guy working the booth says. "Toss the ring and try to get it around the neck of one of the water jugs." There are rows and rows of water jugs with long necks in the center of the booth.

"That sounds really easy. What's the catch?" Melanie asks.

The guy sighs. He probably explains this game a thousand times a day. "No catch. You just can't lean over the counter."

She turns to me. "Okay, chaperone. I'm going to play this until I win one of those." She points to the display above the jugs. Enormous stuffed giraffes and pandas with wires around their necks hang from some fencing. They look like they're being strangled. She puts out her hand for money.

"Wait a minute," I say to the man in the booth. "How many rings does she have to land before she gets a giant panda?"

"Twelve," he replies. He's got a long face and big

teeth. He looks a little like a horse. "It'll only cost you a buck."

"That's if you get all of the rings onto the jugs," I say. "What if you only get one or two?"

"You can walk away with one of the little prizes," he says, and he points to a pile of miniature stuffed animals—blue bunnies and red monkeys. "Or you can keep playing until you get to twelve. You can do it as many times as you want." He's probably hoping we stay there and play just to give him something to do.

"Come on, Goodman," Melanie says. "Hand over some cash so I can win a panda."

"Are you sure?" I ask. "You can go play the water gun game. That's much easier." I point to a booth along the side of the pier. A yellow wooden sign over the booth declares, "A Winner Every Time!"

She grins. Her eyes have a hundred different colors in them. "Wait until you see how fast I win this."

Her confidence convinces me to cough up the money. I peel a bill off the pile, and she pays for four games up front. The horse-faced man seems amused by her. He hands her three red, plastic rings. Then he leans back against the side of the booth and crosses his arms in front of his chest.

The game is not as easy as it looks. Almost every time Melanie tosses a ring, it bounces off of the jugs and lands between the rows. She tosses all twelve and only lands three. "You can keep trying," the man offers.

She squints at him. "I only win one of the monkeys for getting three?"

"Or a bunny. Or you can keep going and get that panda."

She looks over at me, and I put my hands up. "Don't ask me. You already wasted a dollar."

She sighs, and her shoulders rise and fall in the most adorable way. "Okay, I'll just take a monkey." The man liberates one of the red monkeys from its bondage and hands it to her. She considers it with a frown. "You want it?" She holds it out to me. It's the ugliest stuffed animal I've ever seen. It has a tuft of red hair like a mohawk and bulging plastic eyes.

"No, that's all yours." I push it away, but Melanie starts shaking it and forcing it on me. Soon, she's chasing me with this ugly monkey, and we're both laughing and running around the pier. When we finally stop, I'm dizzy just from being near her.

I want to try the squirt gun game, but I think the money Artie gave me is only supposed to be for Melanie. I get change for the dollar bills at a booth near the front of the pier and keep handing her quarters. She plays a bunch of midway games, badly. She can't win a big stuffed animal to save her life. We're down to four bucks by lunchtime. "We'd better slow down," I say, and I slide onto a bench in the shade of a picnic awning. "Your dad wants me to bring him change."

She flops down next to me. "He doesn't care. I could go back and ask him for twenty bucks right now, and he'd give it to me."

"No way! Your dad means business when he says something. I'm going back there with change."

Melanie narrows her eyes at me. "How do you know what my dad means or doesn't mean? You barely know him."

I bite my lip. Of course, she's right. Come to think of it, other than his name, I don't know anything about Artie Bishop.

She slaps at her thighs and stands up. "I'm starving, Goodman. Buy me lunch, Sir Chaperone!" She walks off to find some food. Her ponytail swishes back and forth across her back like a giant paintbrush. I sit there watching her move, my heart beating fast in my chest.

The rest of the day speeds by. At lunch, she eats a cheeseburger. I drink a Coke. I don't eat cheeseburgers. They aren't kosher because they mix milk and meat. It's one of the Jewish laws—that you can't mix dairy and meat at the same meal. I mean, I *could* eat a cheeseburger. It's not like something bad will happen if I do. But I always feel like Bubbe is somehow watching me and judging me. Kind of like God, except I *know* Bubbe's real.

In the afternoon, Melanie and I go on rides until our money runs out. She insists on riding the Tilt-A-Whirl over and over again, and by the time we stagger out of our car for the fifth or sixth time, I feel my brain rattling around inside my skull. Melanie laughs as I teeter off the sloped platform like a drunk.

It's a quarter to four when we leave the pier and head back to Pinky's. I think that this was the best day of my life. Melanie's quiet on our walk back, but she glances at me a couple of times, which is so cool.

"You're sure your dad's not going to mind that we don't have any change?" I ask.

Melanie runs her hand along the railing at the Boardwalk's edge. "Do you ever stop worrying, Goodman? You're like an old man!" She punches my shoulder, and I pretend it really hurts so she'll laugh again. "Look, just let me do the talking when we get back, okay? It'll be fine, I promise." Her nose and forehead are pink from the sun, and her shoulders are flecked with freckles.

When we reach Pinky's, I hold the door for her, and she does a little curtsy, like she's a princess. I follow her back to the bar area, where Artie is seated at a table, deep in conversation with a man sweating his butt off in a light blue linen suit. Artie's minions are not around.

After a minute or two, Artie thumps his knuckles on the table, ending the conversation. The man in the suit mops at his brow, and he looks like he's about to toss his cookies. He thanks Artie about ten times before moving off. When Artie finally sees us, he stands and holds his arms open wide. "You're back!" He looks at his watch. "Four o'clock on the dot! Joey, you're a man who can be trusted." He gently smacks my cheek, like Bubbe does when I've made her proud, before he leans over to give Melanie a peck.

"We had such a good time, Pops," she says, and I can't tell if she's being honest or pulling the wool over his eyes. "You know, the prices really went up on Million Dollar Pier since last summer! Wow! I couldn't believe it. The ten bucks you gave us went in no time."

The prices haven't gone up on Million Dollar Pier since the sixties. I keep this to myself while Melanie plays this little game with her father.

Artie looks back and forth between us. "Did they now?" I try to look sincere, but my stomach drops to the floor. I wait to be interrogated like a prisoner of war. But Artie just says, "I didn't know that. You need a little more tomorrow?"

I croak out, "No!" at the same time as Melanie says, "Yes!" Artie laughs and pats my cheek again.

Tommy the bartender approaches Artie with his eyes down. He's holding a full garbage bag behind his back.

"Artie, think I can have a minute just to, you know, talk to you about that thing?" Tommy looks like he's about Uncle Sol's age or maybe older. He's got long sideburns and a gold tooth in the front of his mouth.

Artie looks him up and down. He hands Melanie a dollar bill and tells her to go play a game in the arcade. To me he says, "Joey, why don't you go throw Tommy's garbage in the dumpster out back? I'm going to talk to him for a minute."

"Uh, okay," I reply, and Tommy hands me the bag. Something tells me I don't want to hear this conversation anyway. I hold the heavy bag away from my body and take it out the back door to the dumpster.

I can't help but smile to myself. Artie's really treating me like I'm one of the guys now, isn't he? I could get used to this!

Out back sits a delivery truck with the words HAMPTON APPLIANCE AND TELEVISION painted on the side in black block letters. The rear door is rolled up, and Ralphie and Grunts stand at the end of a ramp coming off the back of the truck. Ralphie is speaking with someone inside. I set the bag down as quietly as possible and peek around the side of the dumpster.

A scrawny man in a delivery uniform stands in the truck, his shoulders hunched, wiping the back of his neck with a dirty towel. Behind him sit about fifty television sets in boxes, piled on top of one another in neat stacks.

"I want the Zenith console," Ralphie says, pointing to a box on the bottom of one of the stacks. "None of those Sylvania pieces of junk. And one for Artie. And Grunts too." Grunts nods and garbles something to the delivery man.

"But Ralphie," the man pleads, "Mr. Hampton's gonna notice if the big console Zeniths are missing. Can't you just take a small RCA?" He chews on his knuckles and moves his eyes over the sets.

Maybe I shouldn't be seeing this.

Ralphie frowns. "Do not make me come up there, Frank. You don't want me climbing in that truck. Bring down the Zeniths, you hear me?"

Frank mutters, "I'm gonna lose my job."

"You're gonna lose your head if you don't hurry up," Ralphie says. Grunts shakes with laughter.

I don't want to be out here anymore. Sweat runs down my forehead and into my eyes, and I blink a hundred times. I seriously doubt Ralphie and Grunts are going to pay Frank for the TVs.

I turn to go, and I knock the garbage bag by my feet.

The noise makes Ralphie look over. His eyes, clear blue like icicles, drill into mine.

"What are you doin' out here?" he snarls.

I want to answer, but I can't make my voice work. Instead, my mouth freezes in the shape of an O.

Ralphie yells, "Get out of here, kid! Scram!"

My heart thumps so hard in my chest that I'm certain it's going to explode. I don't wait for Ralphie to tell me again. I leave the garbage bag next to the dumpster and make a beeline for the back door.

I rush straight through Pinky's and out to the Boardwalk without saying goodbye to anyone, not even Melanie. Artie had to know what I'd find when I went out there, and he sent me out there anyway. Did he want me to see that?

I stay close to Reuben as I work the dinner shift. When a fork falls, I pick it up. When a water glass empties, I fill it. I try not to twitch at every sudden sound. But the St. Bonaventure is all around me, all solid and sure, and that eases my mind a bit.

Reuben places his hand on my shoulder, and I ask him to repeat whatever he just said to me. He laughs. "I asked if you want to take the dessert orders tonight, squirt."

I gaze up at my brother's friendly face. "Do you think I can?"

"Of course you can. Don't worry. I'll be right there next to you." He hands me his little pad and pen for me to write down the orders.

I move around the tables slowly, and the guests tell me if they want sherbet or chocolate cake for dessert. I nod a lot and write it all down, just the way I've seen Reuben do it. I bring out full trays from the kitchen, and I only have to look at the pad a couple of times to place the right dish in front of every person. When I finish with all four of my tables, the guests clap for me, and I lean into Reuben's hug. From across the dining room, Bubbe beams at me. I smile too, but I have to turn away because my chest is so full and if I look at her any longer, I know I'll cry.

When the guests leave and the tables are clean, I wander to the lobby. I take a seat on a lumpy couch and wait for my brothers to take me to the house. My shoulders sag, and my eyelids droop. Today felt as long as a whole week.

Reuben removes his kippah as he walks into the lobby, and Simon is behind him, shoving a piece of chocolate cake into his mouth. "You ready to go, squirt?" Reuben asks.

"I don't think you should call me that anymore."

"You know what? You're right. You ready to go, Joey?"

The three of us walk toward the back entrance of the hotel, and Simon side-eyes me. "I'm still going to call you squirt, squirt." He opens his mouth wide and shows me his half-eaten cake. What a jerk.

But I'll take Simon's chewed-up chocolate over Ralphie's cold eyes anytime.

CHAPTER 7

Despite my triumphant dessert performance, Ralphie and his frigid eyes haunt my dreams that night. Grunts's creepy laughter too. I wake, sweating, in the deepest hours of the night, and for a minute, I forget where I am. I settle back onto my pillow, but I'm breathing hard.

I have to do a good job as Melanie's chaperone. I have to.

Which means I have to keep lying to my family.

I worry myself into a frenzy about getting out of working the lunch service for the next two weeks. By the time I approach Bubbe in the hotel kitchen on Tuesday, I've come up with a decent story, but I'll have to lie directly to her face. The thought of this has my stomach rumbling like a freight train.

She's in one of the giant pantries, counting the industrial-size cans of crushed tomatoes. I squeak out, "Bubbe?"

She turns her head to me for just a moment before writing a few things on the legal pad she's holding. "What is it, Yussel?" Somehow, hearing her use my

Yiddish name makes me feel worse. Who lies to their grandmother like this?

I sigh before launching into the thick of it. "Bubbe, I was hoping I could just work the breakfast and dinner shifts for the next few weeks because I made some friends out on the beach, and they're really nice, and you'd really like them because they're good Jewish kids whose families are from Lakewood."

As soon as I mention Lakewood, Bubbe's face lights up. Lakewood is a town here in New Jersey with a ton of Orthodox Jews, and if I met kids from Lakewood, she'd automatically approve. "Of course," she says. "Go play with your new friends." Then she tells me to ask Uncle Sol for some money to buy saltwater taffy, which is the only kosher food on the Boardwalk.

When I tell Mom the same story, she's thrilled to let me skip work. I've heard her talking to Dad: "Reuben and Simon had a lot of friends when they were thirteen, and Ben makes friends everywhere he goes, but Joey—*poor Joey*—he's so quiet. It's not healthy!" I wonder if she'd think Melanie is a "healthy" friend.

I'm able to leave the dining room at nine thirty on Tuesday without any problem. On Wednesday, Reuben follows me with his eyes as I head out. I can't remember the last time I lied to Reuben. Well, actually, I lied to him just the other day about having a headache. I give him a quick, guilty wave before I duck my head and scoot off.

But Ben's the one I can't seem to shake. He doesn't have anything on his acting schedule for the week, so he follows me around as I rush to get changed and ready for Melanie. Why he's chosen right now to buddy up to me is a mystery. Maybe Mom's had enough of him for a while and told him to go bug me.

I hustle into Uncle Sol's office to change into shorts, and Ben is attached to me like a housefly I want to swat.

"Get away from me, Beans!" I say as I push him out of the office. "I don't have time for this right now!" I attempt to shut the door, but Ben molds his body around both sides of the doorframe. Shaking my head like Dad would, I grab the ShopRite bag next to the desk and dump my shorts and shirt out on the floor.

"Why are you in such a hurry? Where are you going? You never play with me anymore, Joey." Ben should be in *The Guinness Book of World Records* for whining. He's also an excellent actor. He looks at me with really sad eyes, and for a moment, I forget that he's just bored.

I unbutton my work shirt and stuff it into the bag. "I'm thirteen, Ben. I'm too old to play with you like we used to." I pull on my shirt. It's my best clean shirt, the navy blue one with the collar and the alligator on the pocket. I tell myself I'm not trying to impress Melanie, but I know that's exactly what I'm doing.

Ben lets go of the doorframe and pushes out a dejected sigh. He wipes at his eyes, and either he's worthy of an Academy Award or he's actually crying. I can't tell. In any case, I have to take my pants off, and I'd rather not do that with the office door open so all the old people can look in. I take the Reuben route. "I'll tell you what. Tonight at the house, I'll play you in Monopoly, and you can start off with five hundred extra bucks. How does that sound?" I really do sound like Reuben. Now I wonder if Reuben finds me as annoying as I find Ben.

Ben nods but continues to pull his hands across his eyes. "Okay," he says. I'm about to congratulate myself on being a good big brother when he adds cheerfully, "Plus I get two houses on St. James Place."

I take off a shoe and make like I'm going to toss it at him. "Get out of here, Beans!"

Ben does his best villain laugh and trots off. It's not a big deal, though. I know he can only play Monopoly for about fifteen minutes before he's had enough and goes to watch TV.

I shut the door and quickly change into my shorts and sneakers. I toss my kippah into the bag too. I want to show off my Skee-Ball skills to Melanie today, try to impress her a little. Yesterday, she wanted to go to the beach, so I got to see her in a bathing suit. It was a one-piece suit, but she still looked dynamite. When I'm with her, I forget about Ralphie and Grunts and what I saw on Monday behind Pinky's.

A glance at the clock in the lobby tells me it's ten of ten. I'm aiming for the Boardwalk when Mom practically tackles me by the revolving door. "Again you're going to meet these new friends?" she asks, and she tries to tuck my shirt into my shorts. I bat her hand away.

"Ma, stop! Stop! I gotta go! I'll see you later."

Before she moves aside, she wags a finger at me. "If you meet an Orthodox girl, don't go to shake her hand, understand? The Orthodox don't shake hands with the opposite sex."

I let out a groan, sidestep her, and race out the door.

I hurtle through the front door at Pinky's, sure that I'm a few minutes late, but neither Artie nor Melanie is there. In fact, the restaurant area is empty. Even Tommy the bartender isn't at his usual spot. I sit at one of the empty tables and stare at that back door, thinking about what I saw out there a couple of days ago and how Ralphie barked at me.

I shift on the chair, but I can't find a comfortable way to sit. I'm also sweating right through my good shirt. I try to sniff my underarms because although I put on deodorant, there wasn't much left in the can, and I'm panicked that Melanie is going to think I stink. I have to use the bathroom now.

The men's room at Pinky's, which is not much better than the bathroom at that diner where I first met Artie, is down a short hallway and around a corner. I'm still trying to get a whiff of my underarms as I round the corner, but I look up and stop cold. Ralphie is on the pay phone outside the men's room. All I see is his enormous back straining the seams of a dove-gray sports jacket as he leans against the wall. He mumbles "Mmm-hmm" a few times. Without daring to breathe, I creep back around the corner.

"You don't tell *me* when it's time! I tell *you* when it's time!" Ralphie hisses. "I got everything under control here. Tell Al it's all under control." The person on the other end must be talking because for a moment the only sound is Ralphie's wheezing breath. When he speaks again, the intensity of his voice jolts every sense in my body. "Listen, you tell Al that I'm the one who makes the timeline here! And I expect to be paid. Ten thousand bucks. I'm not doing this for my health." Pause. "No, he doesn't suspect anything! I'm a professional! I'm hanging up now." He bangs the receiver against the wall three times before jamming it back on the cradle.

What was that all about? Every time I come to this place, I see things I shouldn't see and hear things I shouldn't hear. Ralphie is planning something. Something terrible.

Going to the men's room is out of the question now. I flash down the hallway and out into the restaurant. It's still mostly empty, but Melanie is sitting at one of the tables with Eddie. He gnaws on a toothpick and cleans his fingernails while Melanie leans her elbow on the table with her chin in her hand. She looks half asleep. Her hair hangs in a long, loose braid. She wears a faded blue T-shirt with pink hearts ironed on the front, and she scuffs her flip-flops back and forth on the wood floor. I make my way over to the table. When she sees me, she brightens, so I brighten too.

"Hey, Goodman!" she says. She kicks a chair out from the table. "Have a seat. Eddie here is seeing us off today." She points at him with her thumb and rolls her eyes.

"Oh, okay." I squeeze my fists in the pockets of my shorts. I would like to get out of here before Ralphie comes back.

Eddie glances at me but still seems more interested in his fingernails. "Artie said no funny business and be back by four."

"Like every day." She fake-smiles at him, but he doesn't see her do it. I guess she doesn't like being pawned off on Eddie. "Did my dad say to give us money?" She puts her hand out, and Eddie stops his self-manicure long enough to fish a few bills out of the pocket of his jacket.

"You don't gotta be a brat about it," he says to her.

Someone grasps my shoulders from behind, and I let out a Chihuahua yelp. Ralphie laughs and squeezes harder. "Good-man! You're jumpy this morning! You feelin' all right?" He spins me around so I'm facing him. I expect to see the frigid eyes that I saw by the TV truck on Monday, but that's not what I see at all. Ralphie's eyes are vibrant and warm, and there's no trace of cruelty on his face. Which concerns me even more. I move my head around, and my neck cracks.

"I'm good, thanks." I turn to Melanie. "You want to go?"

As we walk toward the entrance, Ralphie calls after us. "Be safe out there, kids! There's a lot of bad guys around!"

You're not kidding. I look over my shoulder. I mean to check his eyes again before I go. But he's already turned away, and I'm a little relieved.

★ ★ ★

"You don't want to go to Steel Pier," I say with a warning shake of my head.

"Yeah, I do! I haven't been there for a couple of years. It was always so much fun!"

She doesn't understand. "It's not fun anymore, not like Million Dollar Pier. There's hardly anything left on Steel Pier."

Melanie refuses to accept this. "The diving horses are still there, right? And the water show? I'm sure there's plenty of other stuff to do. You said yourself that you don't go there anymore. So how do you know what's there anyway?"

She's sort of right. I haven't gone to Steel Pier at all in the last two or three years. My parents won't let me. Uncle Sol told me a teenager was robbed at gunpoint on Steel Pier in broad daylight back in '72. I know Uncle Sol's stories are usually only half true, but I'm not taking any chances. I put my head down and mutter to my feet, "Can we just do something else?"

"You don't want to see the ape woman. You don't want to go to Steel Pier. You're a worse chaperone than Eddie!" She throws her hands up.

Her words sting like a shot from the doctor's office. The truth is, I'm scared to go to Steel Pier, scared of the people, scared of what might happen there. I let out a long sigh. I'm living up to everything my family thinks about me. Again.

"Fine," I say, my cheeks burning. "Let's go."

Overflowing trash cans flank the entrance to Steel Pier, but we pay for two whole-day passes and go through the gates that lead onto the pier from the Boardwalk. We walk through a long, narrow building with display cases lining the blank walls. Some of the cases are empty. Others display weird memorabilia from Steel Pier's better days. I spot Rex the Wonder Dog's waterskiing board. There's a tiny boxing ring and boxing gloves that used to fit on the paws of the boxing cats. In one case, the empty two-person costume of Spark Plug the horse hangs from wires, the painted cloth face staring out like a gargoyle. My hair lifts off the back of my neck. The walls and ceiling press down on us.

Melanie says, "I feel like we're in a trash compactor."

The building goes on forever. We pass vacant game booths, a movie theater, a tourist shop selling Steel Pier snow globes. People wander around with quiet, confused faces, wondering if they're in the right place. The floor is covered in smashed cigarette butts and discarded peanut shells.

When we finally exit the building, we're at the back of the pier near the water show area. We take a seat in the stands with about twenty other people and wait for the show to start. "I thought the diving boards would be much higher," Melanie says as she squints into the sun.

An announcer tries to drum up some enthusiasm from the stands as he goes on about what we're going to see. In front of the diving pool, a kid spills a bag of pop-corn, and the wind scatters the kernels across the ground. Finally, five men in tiny bathing suits come out from under a striped tent and walk onto the deck of the diving pool. They wave to the crowd and receive a smattering of applause.

"They look bored," Melanie whispers to me.

The men dive from boards of varying heights, flip-ping and twirling in the air before landing hard in the pool. The divers who are in the Olympics on TV are way better than these guys. A couple does an aerial act, spinning around like tops from a trapeze about thirty feet above the pool. Melanie and I side-eye each other when a person in a bear costume comes out on a unicycle.

"Wow," she says. We leave the stands and drift toward the diving horse area until scuffling noises to our left make us turn off our path.

Ahead of us, people gather in a small circle. A cou-ple of men's voices call out. "Get him, Don! Get him!" "Show him who's boss!" In the center of the circle, two men around my dad's age are locked together, throwing punches, growling. The bystanders are silent and still, like they're observing lab rats. The men's friends shuffle around the circle, cheering on their pals, jeering at the others, until two Boardwalk cops finally show up and wrestle the men apart.

"Let's skip the diving horses," Melanie says with a sigh. "I suddenly don't want to watch a horse slide into a pool of water from twenty feet up. It's too pathetic. I'll just cry." I press my hands to my stomach and nod in agreement.

We play some midway games and don't win anything. We go to the theater and watch an Abbott and Costello movie that I've seen a hundred times. It's the one where they meet Frankenstein. Lou Costello makes goofy faces and bumps into things, and Melanie and I chuckle halfheartedly.

Now there's nothing left to do. I can't believe I was afraid to come here this morning. Steel Pier isn't scary; it's just sad.

Melanie and I don't talk as we walk back through the dreary building to the pier's entrance gate. I follow her as she starts down the boards. We just walk and walk. Neither of us will say what we're both thinking: that something we used to love is dying, and we have no power to bring it back.

"How come you don't eat anything when I get lunch?" she asks as we stand in line at Nathan's Hot Dogs. "Aren't you starving by four?"

"I'm starving right now. But I'll get a Coke, and that'll fill me up for a while."

"Why not get a hot dog or some fries?"

I sigh. "They're not kosher."

"That's a Jewish thing, right? Pops said you're Jewish." We move up a few steps. "So you can't eat hot dogs?"

I slip off my shoe and turn it over. A pebble falls out along with some sand. Somehow, even if you don't go down to the beach, you still end up with sand in your shoes. "I can eat kosher hot dogs." I pound my shoe against my palm to make sure the sand is all out.

Melanie squints at me. "A hot dog's a hot dog, isn't it?"

"You really don't know?" I squeeze my foot back into the sneaker and take off the other one.

"How would I know? You're the first Jewish person I've ever really talked to."

I stop mid-pound.

"I mean, I don't hang out with any Jewish kids at school," she continues. "I don't even know if there are Jewish kids at my school. Maybe they just blend in with the regular kids."

I examine my shoelaces for a moment. "We *are* regular kids."

Melanie waves her hand in the air. "You know what I mean."

"Not really." I drop my sneaker to the boards and shove my foot inside it.

Melanie stammers. "I–I'm sorry, Goodman. I shouldn't have said that. I wasn't thinking."

"It's okay," I say, even though it's kind of not.

We're at the front of the line now, so Melanie orders her food and a Coke for me. She pays with the money Eddie gave her. I should be the one holding the money, but I guess it doesn't really matter.

We sit at a round picnic table in the little pavilion next to Nathan's. A man in a Phillies cap has a ball game playing on a transistor radio a few tables away. My stomach growls, and I look around to see if anyone can hear it besides me. Melanie's french fries look kind of soggy, but I'll bet they taste pretty good. I'm not going to make it until four o'clock.

"So, where do you and your mom live?" I keep my eyes on Melanie's face to distract me from her food.

She sips her soda. Even the way her lips wrap around a straw is cute. "Is today the day for asking me questions, Goodman?"

Heat rushes to my cheeks. "I was just making conversation."

She shifts around on the bench. "It's fine. I'm only kidding. I live in Hackensack."

"You live in New Jersey?"

"Yeah. Where'd you think I lived?"

I shrug. "I don't know. Farther away. Your dad said he doesn't see you that much."

"That's because Mom hates him. She doesn't want me to see him."

"That stinks."

She chews on a fry. "They always fought. They used to yell at each other all the time, even after they got divorced. Now we live far enough away that they just talk about each other behind each other's backs."

I can't imagine my parents behaving that way. Their fights are pretty rare. I can't even recall a time when I heard my father yell at my mother. Mom gets aggravated if Dad forgets to flush the toilet or put his dirty towels in the hamper, but that's about it. Whenever my mom does raise her voice, Dad leaves the room, and Mom gets on the phone and calls Bubbe.

We're quiet for a minute before she says, "Anything else you want to know?"

There is. "The other day, Ralphie called your dad the king of Steel Pier. What did he mean by that?"

She wipes each of her hands with her napkin and crumples it up. "Want to go walk on the beach?" she asks, and she gets up to toss away her trash.

"Uh, okay." I guess she's not going to answer that question.

* * *

It's still cloudy as we walk along the shore, but the threat of rain has passed. The sun peeks through here and there. My sneakers dangle from my fingers, my socks tucked inside. Melanie holds her flip-flops too. New Jersey sand isn't like sand in other places, like Florida. My parents and my brothers and I sometimes go to Florida over winter vacation, and the beach down there is dotted with palm trees, and the sand is soft and white. The sand in Atlantic City is rougher, coarser. And the ocean is always chilly, even in August.

Melanie picks up a shell and examines it before letting it drop back onto the sand.

"My dad is a war veteran. Did you know that?"

"No, I had no idea."

"Yup. Korean War. He has a Purple Heart and everything. He was shot in the leg."

I don't know what to say. I don't know anyone who fought in the Korean War. In fact, I only know one or two people who fought in Vietnam, and that war just ended.

"That's how he met my mom. She was a nurse at the military hospital he went to." She stops for a moment and digs her big toe into the sand. "I had a brother, you know. I had a brother named Chris. He died in Vietnam in 1970. He was eighteen, and he'd been there for less than a month." She makes another hole with her toe, and another, and another.

"Wow, I'm sorry," I say, which probably doesn't help. What's the right way to react when someone tells you something like that?

"That's when my parents started fighting all the time, after Chris died. Mom took me to live near my grandparents in Hackensack." She shrugs. "It's not bad up there. It's different than living down the shore, but it's been a few years, so I'm pretty used to it by now."

We start walking again, moving slowly along the edge of the water. "My dad grew up down here in Atlantic City," she says. "He's been here all his life. When he was young, he worked on Steel Pier."

"Really?"

"Yup. He was a really good swimmer, and he was in the water show. Swam around, dove off the high dive and stuff. He was so handsome back then. I've seen the pictures. He was . . . dashing, you know what I mean?"

"I can see that," I say with a nod, and I can.

"He was like a celebrity on Steel Pier. He even went onstage with Frank Sinatra once in the old Marine Ballroom."

"Get outta here!"

She nods. "He did! He didn't sing or anything, but Sinatra called him up onstage one time because they were like buddies."

I picture Artie, young, carefree . . . a Jersey boy, just like Frank Sinatra himself, standing on the stage, waving to the packed house . . . the lights of Steel Pier dazzling at night . . .

She finds another shell and turns it over in her hands. "I used to collect stuff from the beach when I was little," she says. "I had a whole jelly jar filled with shells and things. I wonder what happened to it." She tosses the shell into the water that laps at our feet.

My toes brush at the sand, and I find a shard of blue sea glass, its edges rubbed smooth from the ocean. I hand it to Melanie, and she wraps her fingers around it like it's a pearl.

"He didn't go to college or anything," she continues. "None of his pals did. He went to war. He went to Korea. Then he came back, and he fell in with some guys . . ." She waves her hand as if to shoo away the men she's talking about. "But he was smarter than the rest of them, you know?"

She starts walking again. "So, my dad, he's back from Korea, and he starts moving up in his . . ." She searches for the right word. ". . . organization, and they're all out one night, on Steel Pier, dancing and drinking and all. And my dad's boss says something about my mother. I don't know what it was, but I guess it was pretty gross. And he was the boss, so my dad was supposed to just take it and not say anything back. But he didn't. He beat the guy up right there on Steel Pier."

She stops and faces me. The wind off the ocean roars in my ears. "And everyone watched, and no one said a thing or tried to stop him. And then he became the boss. That's why Ralphie called him the king of Steel Pier. Because that night, he overthrew the king and became the king himself." She swallows hard and picks at her lip with her thumbnail. "I only know about that because I overheard Eddie telling someone the story. My dad would never tell me that story. Look, I know who my father is. He's probably done some bad stuff. But he's still my dad, and I love him."

I blink at her. I don't know what I expected Artie's story to be, but it wasn't this. I thought maybe he'd won some contest or something, some prize, and he was crowned the king of Steel Pier. Now I can't believe how ridiculous that sounds.

My lips are dry from the sea salt in the air. I lick them, but that doesn't help. "Can we sit down for a minute? I'm a little . . . dizzy."

Melanie takes my wrist and pulls me up the beach. She finds an abandoned hotel towel and makes me sit.

"You need something to eat, Goodman. The ice cream man is right there." She points off to my left. "I'm getting you an ice cream, and I don't care if it's not kosher or whatever!" She takes my silence as agreement and stalks off.

Artie did want me to catch Ralphie and Grunts taking those TVs off that truck. He wanted me to understand his power, to see his strength. Maybe a few weeks ago, I would've said that there's more than one way to show you're strong, but now, Artie's idea of strength is very convincing. He doesn't have to do the heavy lifting himself anymore, like he used to. His guys do all that for him now. He really is the king of Steel Pier. And Ralphie and Grunts and Eddie? They're like his knights. They'll do whatever he asks them to do. What does that make me?

Melanie returns with two ice cream sandwiches. She unwraps one and hands it to me, and I'm too spent to worry about whether it's kosher. She sits down next to me, unwraps the other one, and bites it with a grunt. This makes us both laugh, and I take a big bite too.

She leans into me. "You didn't know what you were getting yourself into with this chaperone thing, did you?" She licks the ice cream around the edges of the sandwich.

"No, not at all," I say. The sandwich isn't that great, but I've never enjoyed ice cream more.

"Well, if it makes you feel any better, my dad likes you."

"He does? How do you know that?"

"He said so. He likes working with Jewish people. He says Jews are real smart." Not all of us. I could introduce her to some of my friends who are complete boneheads.

Melanie scrunches up her eyes at me. "So, Jews think Jesus was good. They just don't think he's God, right?"

I lick the pads of my fingers to get the chocolate off them. "Jesus doesn't come up in our conversations."

"Really?" She lets this sink in as she pops the last bite of ice cream into her mouth. "But Jesus is, like, the whole Bible."

"Not our Bible."

She shakes her head. "I don't think I could ever be Jewish. You have all these rules about what you can and can't eat. Your Bible is different, and your God is different. Sounds confusing."

It can be. At least that's how it seems lately. Still, I feel the need to defend my people. "If you've been doing it your whole life, you get used to it. I mean, it's who I am, so . . ."

Melanie shrugs and crumples up her wrapper. Something on the waxy paper catches my eye.

"Look at that!" I say, pointing to a small mark on the packaging. "There's a circled K on the ice cream."

"What's that mean?"

"The ice cream's kosher."

Melanie smiles at me. I'd love to kiss her right now. I'm too scared to try, though. Guess I'm not ready to be her knight just yet.

* * *

Later, at Bubbe and Zeyde's house, Ben makes me break out Monopoly. He grabs for the plastic bag of game pieces. "I want to be the thimble!" And just as I predicted, he's fidgeting by the time his piece has gone around the board twice. He trots off to the living room to watch TV, and I get the box back out.

"Don't put it away, squirt. You still want to play?" It's Simon, and he sits at the kitchen table across from me. "I'll take over for Beans." I hesitate. I'm still imagining him snarling at me in Uncle Sol's backyard.

"I'm the bank," I say, thinking he's going to argue.

"Okay. What am I, the thimble? Beans always wants to be the thimble." He starts organizing his multicolored money. "Whose turn is it, yours?"

I stare at him for a moment. Who is this person sitting across from me? "Yeah, my turn." I pick up the dice and shake them in my hands.

Mom comes down the steps in her nightgown and

robe. "You're playing Monopoly without me? I don't think so!" She takes a chair and rubs her hands together. "You boys ready to get whipped by your mother?" She rifles through the leftover tokens and chooses the race car. "Okay, let's get going here!" She glares at me with mock impatience. "Well, banker? Can I have my money, please?"

The three of us play for hours, haggling and joking around the whole time. Mom is ruthless. By midnight, I'm bankrupt, and all Simon has left is a hundred bucks and one hotel on Baltic Avenue. But no one cares, and Mom gives us each a kiss on the head before she goes upstairs. I wish I could take a picture of this moment and hold on to it.

When I finally get into bed, I think about Simon being nice to me and how my mom makes things fun sometimes. But soon my thoughts turn to Artie's strong hand on my shoulder and Melanie's smile.

It's like I'm standing on a fence post, and I don't know how long I can keep my balance.

CHAPTER 8

Reuben is definitely getting suspicious. He watches me leave the dining room each morning before the breakfast shift is even over, and he watches me come back to the St. Bonaventure after four o'clock, sweaty and breathless from my time away. I usually tell Reuben everything, but Melanie is not a secret to share. I don't *really* lie to him, not like I did to Bubbe and Mom. I'm just omitting the truth. I'm omitting the truth to Reuben and Simon and Zeyde and Uncle Sol and . . . okay, I'm lying. But it's not hurting anyone, right? I've almost forgotten that I'm getting paid to spend time with Mel. At this point, I'd do the job for free.

On Friday afternoon, we're headed back toward Pinky's for the final check-in of the week. I'm about to tell Melanie what a great time I've had when she points to someone leaning against the railing across the Boardwalk from Pinky's. "That guy over there is staring at us, Goodman. Do you know him?" My head snaps up, and my jaw goes slack when I see who she's pointing to.

Reuben stands there, his white waiter's shirtsleeves

rolled up to his elbows, one foot crossed over the other, watching us walk toward him. Questions crowd my brain, but the most important one is the one I ask as soon as we stop in front of him, without even introducing him to Melanie: "What are you doing here?"

"Nice to see you too." He reaches out his hand for Melanie to shake. "I'm Reuben, Joey's older brother."

When I look over at Melanie, I do a double take. She may as well be drooling. She's shaking Reuben's hand, but you'd think she was looking at Burt Reynolds. "I'm Melanie Bishop," she says, "Joey's friend."

They're shaking hands for too long. "Reuben, what are you doing here?"

Reuben keeps his eyes on Melanie as he answers me. "I wanted to meet your Orthodox friends from Lakewood."

"Huh?" Melanie says.

"Nothing," I mutter. "Wait—did you follow us all day?"

Reuben laughs. It's a charming, easy laugh, and I actually hate him a little right now. "No! I followed you here this morning to see what you were really up to, and then after you left with Melanie, I went inside and spoke to her dad. He said you'd be back at four. We had a nice conversation."

No. This cannot be happening. My worlds are colliding.

A bead of sweat swims down my face from my temple to my chin.

"Joey's told me a lot about you," Melanie says. "You're his idol." She's mooning over him like he's her idol too. Reuben grins at her. I want to throw up.

"We should go in," I say. "Okay, see you back at the hotel, Reub!" I tug on Melanie's sleeve, but she doesn't even feel it.

"You go ahead. I'll be right in."

"Your dad wants us both in there at four." My voice cracks on the word *both*. I could die right here.

"It'll be fine," she replies. "Just tell him I'm out here talking to your brother. He won't mind."

She smiles at me like I'm a little boy. I sigh and head toward the door. I look back at them as I swing it open, and now Melanie leans her hip against the railing, right next to my brother. He points to the shell-bead bracelet she bought today at a cheap gift shop across from Million Dollar Pier. Melanie holds her wrist up to him and turns her arm so her palm faces up. I have to look away.

Inside, Artie is playing cards with Eddie and two other men I've never seen before. They both have leathery faces and olive skin. As soon as he sees me, Artie waves me over.

"Joey!" he calls out, and the two men glance at me with severe expressions. I pull up a chair next to Artie, and he folds his cards on the table in front of him. "Where's my girl?"

"She's right outside. She'll be in in a minute."

"I met your brother Reuben this morning."

"Yeah, he told me. He's out there talking to Mel right now."

Artie takes a long sip from a beer he lifts from an adjacent table. He places it back down on the coaster and wipes at his lips. "I didn't know you'd told your family about our arrangement."

My stomach tenses. "I—I didn't. I didn't tell anyone."

"I'm out, fellas," he says to the other men. They grunt and keep their eyes on their cards. Artie stands and motions me over to a table closer to the back door. He snaps his fingers in the air and calls out, "Tommy, bring Joey a Coke!" A moment later, Tommy sets a tall glass of soda down in front of me. Artie leans his forearms on the table. "So, you finished a whole week with my girl, and she didn't give you the slip once."

"Yeah, she told me about last summer with Eddie."

Artie grins. "I'm sure she did. She likes to tell that story." We laugh. "But you did a good job this week. You kept her out of trouble, which Eddie couldn't do." I want to ask what kind of trouble he means, but I think I already know. I saw her a minute ago with Reuben. "What did we say, twenty bucks for the week?"

We said thirty. There's no way he doesn't remember that. I'd settle for twenty. Heck, I'd settle for a pat on the back, but ever since I lost my Skee-Ball money, I've been thinking about this payday. "Um, well . . ."

Artie ruffles my hair. "I know, I know. Thirty. Thirty bucks. A good week's take." He pulls a bundle of bills out of his pant pocket and counts out three tens on the tabletop. I don't reach for it right away, almost like I can't believe it's real money. "Go ahead, kid. It's your money."

I take the bills in my hands. The tens are crisp, new. I'll have to find a better place to hide them this time.

"There you go," Artie says. "You have any plans for the weekend? You going dancing or anything?"

I feel my cheeks flush. "No, just working at the hotel and hanging out with my family."

"Your brother Reuben is a polite boy. He learned that from your parents, right?"

I never thought about this before. I shrug. "My parents and my grandparents."

"They're hardworking people, your grandparents."

"Really hardworking."

He nods. "You look up to them?"

"Yeah, I do."

"So, they live over in Margate, right?"

"Mm-hmm," I say. "I mean, we take over the house in August, but it's their house."

A weird, bland smile comes over Artie's face. After a moment, he asks, "And your grandparents' house, it's a big house?"

"It's not that big. I mean, it's not tiny. It's just a regular-size house. Four bedrooms. And they converted the garage into a big storage room."

"Oh, yeah? What's in there?"

I scratch at my neck. I'm surprised he's so interested in this. "Hotel dishes, an old set of encyclopedias, some leftover furniture. Stuff like that."

Artie nods slowly. After a moment he says, "It sounds like you have a very nice family, Joey. Your grandparents, your brothers. Very nice."

My scalp prickles. I bite the inside of my cheek.

Melanie arrives at Artie's side, without Reuben. "Hello, sweetheart," he says.

She kisses his temple. "Hey, Pops."

"Did you have a good week with the Good-man?"

She grins at me. "Much better chaperone than Eddie." She puts out her hand for me to slap her five, which is not the gesture I'd like most from her, but what do I expect? A kiss on the cheek when her father's right there? I take what I can get.

"Is Reuben still outside?" I ask her.

She reaches up and runs her fingers through her hair. "He's waiting for you."

I ask Artie, "Is it all right if I go?"

He doesn't answer right away. Finally, he says, "Sure, kid. You go have a good weekend with your family, okay?"

"Thanks." I stand up and pat my pocket to make sure the money hasn't leaped out on its own. I shift from foot to foot and glance at Melanie.

"Bye, Joey," she says.

"Bye."

Out on the Boardwalk, Reuben waits for me. He rolls his shirtsleeves down when he sees me, covering something written in pen on the inside of his forearm. My mouth drops open. It's a phone number, Melanie's phone number.

I bend down to tie my sneaker, which is not in need of retying. Did she give him her number or did he ask for it? I can't believe he'd ask for it. He's got a girlfriend! But why would she just give it to him? Maybe I'm wrong. Maybe it's not her phone number. Maybe it's something else entirely, like the address for the shop where she bought the bracelet. Yeah, maybe he wants to buy one for Hannah. Or it's his work hours that he wrote on his arm to remind himself. It must be something like that, right?

"You want to tell me about this?" Reuben asks, and he gestures at Pinky's with his chin.

"No, not really."

We start back toward the St. Bonaventure. After a minute or two, he says, "Do you know anything about this guy Artie? Who is he? What does he do for a living?" I keep my eyes focused on the boards and their endless pattern. "Joey, maybe you should—"

"You don't run my life!" I spit out and stop in my tracks.

Reuben draws back and raises his eyebrows at me. "I never said I did, squirt. I just don't think you know what you're doing with these people."

"I know what I'm doing!" What am I so angry about? My throat constricts. "And stop calling me squirt!" I stomp off, but he catches up with me, and we continue our walk in silence. Eventually, I can't take it anymore. "Is that Melanie's phone number written on your arm?"

Reuben sighs, like I'm just a kid and it's none of my business. "Yes."

"What about Hannah?"

"It's just a phone number, squir—uh, Joey. It's not a big deal." We reach the hotel, and I can't wait to get away from him.

"So you're going to cheat on Hannah?" Why am I about to cry?

"Melanie wrote it on my arm. I didn't ask her to."

"But you didn't stop her either."

He jumps in front of me and holds his hand to my chest, forcing me to stop again. "Come on, Joey! It's just a phone number. It's not like I'm getting married. I'm only seventeen!"

I smack his hand down.

"You need to be very careful with those people, Joey. I'm serious! You're not one of them."

Now I look him square in the eyes. "How would you know what I am?" I yank the hotel door open, and something pops in my shoulder. The pain shoots down my arm, but I trudge inside without looking back at him. Hot tears blur my vision, so I wouldn't be able to see him anyway.

★ ★ ★

It irritates me that no one even notices what a bad mood I'm in Friday night. I bang doors shut. I huff and grumble every time I'm asked to do anything. I even skip Shabbat services in the hotel ballroom to sit in a corner and sulk. But all of Mom and Dad's focus is on Ben, who's had three bloody noses in the past two days. Mom thinks the world is coming to an end.

"The pediatrician won't answer my calls on the weekend," she says. Ben's head is tilted back, but the blood dribbles out. Mom holds a towel against his face while she sits at Bubbe's kitchen table.

"Mom, you're suffocating me!" Ben's voice is muffled, but it's still his trademark whine.

Dad examines him from different angles, like Ben's a statue in a museum. "Benjamin, are you sure you didn't hit your nose on something recently?"

"No! I told you that a hundred times!"

Simon comes into the kitchen and shuffles through the pantry. "You know, he picks his nose constantly. That's probably why it bleeds so much."

"I do not!" Ben cries.

"You do so. You get your finger way up there."

Dad glares at him. "Simon, that's enough!"

But Simon is having fun now. "That's what you should take him to the doctor for. Persistent nose-picking." He grabs a box of crackers and shakes it to see if there are any left.

"Mommy, make him stop!"

"Why don't *you* stop?" I mutter on my way to the stairs. It's not that I'm defending Simon. I can't take *any* of them anymore.

Mom calls to me as I climb up to my room. "Joseph, you'd better adjust that attitude, young man!" Her voice echoes up the stairs and into my brain.

I don't reply. I go into my room and shut the door hard. My shoulder is killing me since I pulled it. I'd ask my parents for aspirin, but they'd just give me that disgusting chewable stuff that tastes like orange chalk. I flop down on my cot, roll onto my side, and stare at the wallpaper. It's covered in cartoonish drawings of old pirate maps and characters from *Treasure Island*. This used to be Uncle Sol's room, and I can tell the wallpaper's been here since long before he moved out twenty years ago. It's peeling everywhere, and I can see the older wallpaper pattern of tiny red and pink flowers underneath in some places. My grandparents must've papered right over the flowers with the pirates. I wonder how many more layers are hiding under there.

I wish I didn't care that Melanie gave Reuben her phone number. I wish I didn't care that Reuben let her. I wish I didn't care whether Simon is nice or mean to me. I wish I didn't care what my family thinks of me. I wish I didn't care if Reuben was right that I'm not really one of Artie's guys. I wish I didn't care about the ceramic frogs in the St. Bonaventure's fountain. I wish I didn't care about all the little things people say about Jews. I wish I didn't care whether I believe in God or not.

But I care about all of those things, all of them. Maybe that makes me weak. Artie would say it does, I'm sure. But I can't help it.

A little while later, Ben screams, "Stop it, Simon! Mom! Simon's being mean to me!"

Dad says, "For God's sake, Simon, can't you leave him alone?"

I hear all of this through the closed door because no one in my family understands the concept of speaking at a normal volume. With a sigh, I push myself up off the cot. But as I reach for the doorknob, I lean my forehead against the door. I just have to get through the weekend, and then I can see Melanie again on Monday.

★ ★ ★

On Sunday morning, Reuben and Simon both leave the house to go who-knows-where. They say they're going to play basketball at the Jewish community center, since they have the day off, but they could be lying. I'm not speaking to Reuben anyway, so it doesn't matter to me where they're going.

Dad asks me if I want to sit out on the front porch with him while he does some paperwork. "It's a beautiful day. Bring out that book you're always reading." I'm kind of stunned, and I look around to see if he's actually speaking to someone else. "Don't act so surprised! I can't sit on the porch with my son?"

I shrug and go to the kitchen to get the sports section of the newspaper. I'd rather be practicing my swing or tossing a ball around, but at least this is something.

I slump into an old patio chair next to my father. The cushions on these things are as flat as the grilled-cheese sandwiches that Bubbe makes sometimes. They're practically horizontal lines.

For twenty minutes, I read the box scores from yesterday's baseball games. Dad focuses on his papers. He asked me to come out here with him, but he doesn't seem to have anything to say to me. My mood darkens a little more.

A big white car starts down our street from the corner, its radio blaring Frank Sinatra. It's a white Cadillac, one of those old ones that's as huge as a cruise ship. The top's down, and the red leather seats stand out like splashes of blood. I go over to the porch railing and watch the car come toward the house. When it's a few houses away, my heartbeat quickens.

Ralphie is behind the wheel.

The car's creeping down the street at about five miles an hour.

"I like Sinatra as much as the next guy, but who wants to listen to him that loud?" Dad says as the Caddy slides toward us.

Ralphie turns his head and looks right at me. His eyes lock onto mine, and I'm frozen in place. His glare is a warning: *I know where your family lives, Good-man.* Sinatra's smooth voice gives way to the big band, and Ralphie offers me a nod so slight I almost miss it. He's going by in slow motion; the car is barely moving.

I bound down the front steps, toward the street, but Ralphie steps on the gas, and the car streaks away, around the corner, out of sight. I turn to my dad, but his head is still down. He didn't see. I gulp in air like I've broken the crest of a wave.

I have no idea why this just happened, but I do know that I brought him here. I brought that man to this house, to where my family sleeps at night.

It's eighty-five degrees out, and I shiver.

That afternoon, we're all packed into Bubbe and Zeyde's house, but today the house feels like it's the size of a hamster cage. I can't move without bumping into my uncle or my grandmother or one of my brothers. I ask Zeyde if the air-conditioning is broken about ten times. It's not just me. Everyone's giving each other sideways looks, like we're a band of criminals and we don't trust one another.

Ben is completely unaware of everyone's mood, of course. There was a show about gorillas on TV this morning, so he's spending the day pretending to be an ape. You'd think he was five years old, not ten. He drags his knuckles on the floor and beats his chest and makes ridiculous "Ooo-oo, ahh-ahh" noises.

"Benjamin, calm down!" Mom yells. "I don't want you getting any more nosebleeds!" What nosebleeds have to do with pretending to be a gorilla, I have no idea. Naturally, Ben ignores her and rams into her legs a few times with his head. He's grating on my nerves like nobody's business.

Uncle Sol turns on the TV and settles himself on the couch with a grunt. When the Phillies game comes on, Dad and Reuben and Simon and I try to find places for ourselves near the TV, but we end up crowding behind the coffee table, on the couch, and on the floor. Ben tries to sit on Dad's lap. Once Ben plants himself on someone, he expects all their attention, but Dad sets him aside like he's an annoying pet. So Ben starts his gorilla routine again, jumping on Reuben and Simon and generally behaving like a total pain in the neck.

"Can't you go bug Mom?" Simon asks after he's pulled Ben off of him for the tenth time. "Seriously, Beans, you're a menace!"

Ben stands on the six inches of available couch cushion and puts his fists on his hips. "I am Benace the Menace!" Simon pushes him, and he falls forward and bangs his arm on the coffee table. This starts some obnoxiously loud howls of pain, but at least Ben runs off to the kitchen to get some sympathy from Mom.

Zeyde is doing his usual shuffling around the house with his hands behind his back. He's lived in America for decades but has never really gotten into American sports. I can see that he wants to be with us, though, so he stands next to the couch and tries to get involved in the game, squinting at the screen through his Coke-bottle-thick glasses. Sometimes when I look over, he's rocking back and forth and humming to himself. Everyone else stares at the television screen.

Somewhere around the fourth inning, my mom comes into the room and announces, "We have a Hadassah meeting in fifteen minutes." By "we" she means Bubbe and herself. Hadassah is the Jewish women's group that raises money for Israel.

"Congratulations," Simon mutters, and Mom hits the roof.

"You know what, Simon? I am so sick of this hostility! You are constantly disrespectful, and I've had it!"

Dad says, "Honey, calm down. We're trying to watch the game."

Mom goes over to the TV and switches it off with a flourish. We all gaze at her like she's done some kind of magic trick. "You!" she yells, pointing at Dad. "You let him get away with talking to me like this!"

Dad stands and holds his hands up in front of him. "Where's this coming from, Judy?"

"Don't 'Judy' me!"

Reuben goes over to Mom and puts his arm around her shoulder. "Ma, you're getting yourself so worked up . . ."

She moves away from Reuben like he's hit her. "I am not worked up!"

Ben runs into the room and smacks Simon across the head.

Now everyone is up and shouting. Uncle Sol tries to calm my mother, but that only makes Mom more enraged. Dad keeps saying he doesn't understand why she's upset in the first place. Simon squishes Ben's face into the carpeting, which causes him to wave his arms around like a maniac and knock over a dish of candy. Reuben tries to break up their fight.

Finally, Bubbe plows into the room and screams over everyone, "Stop this! Stop! Right now!" We all turn to her. "Do you hear yourselves? You're all going at each other, and Zeyde is in the kitchen mumbling to himself . . ." She mashes her lips together and starts breathing like an angry giant. My grandfather comes out of the kitchen, his expression grim.

Uncle Sol smiles down at Bubbe. "Mom, everything's fine. You and Judy just go to your meeting, and don't worry about a thing."

"Could you be any more condescending, Sol?" Mom says.

"Don't speak to me like I'm a child!" Bubbe shakes a finger in Uncle Sol's face. "You think you can push me off to my meeting and hide things from me? You think I don't know about your secret?"

Uncle Sol throws his arms up. "What secret? What am I hiding from you, Ma?"

"Men from the casinos come to look at the St. Bonaventure, and you don't tell me? I have to find out from my grandson that you're talking to the casinos?" She points at Reuben, and the color drains from his face.

Dad spins on Reuben. "You told your bubbe about the man from the casino?"

"I asked her who the man was in the lobby with Uncle Sol," Reuben says. "How am I supposed to know that it's some big secret you're keeping from her?"

Uncle Sol rubs Bubbe's arm. "It's a complicated situation, Ma, and I didn't want you to worry about it."

"You didn't want me to worry? It's my hotel too!" Bubbe hollers, and the room erupts again. Everyone is shouting over one another. It's like homeroom before the bell rings. Zeyde looks like he just ate a lemon. Bubbe pounds her open palm with her fist and argues with Uncle Sol. Mom yells at Simon, but he keeps walking away from her. Dad and Reuben get into it over what he revealed to Bubbe. And Ben stands in the middle of the room crying his eyes out.

What is going on with my family? Do I know these people?

I want to disappear into the wall like a ghost. What if they knew *my* secrets, what I've gotten them into?

The doorbell rings, and everyone goes still.

Dad groans, crosses to the door, and throws it open. The door blocks the visitor from our view in the living room, but Dad says, "What the—?"

We hear a young girl's voice, barely above a whisper. "Is Simon here?"

Simon's eyes go wide, and he rushes to the door. The rest of us follow him into the entryway in one mass, like a school of fish. Standing there in the doorway is Farrah, her face swollen and stained with tears. She hugs herself and trembles.

We all stare at her, dumbfounded.

Simon reaches for her. "What happened?"

He gathers Farrah in his arms and walks her to the kitchen. We hear him help her into a chair, go into the fridge, crack open a can of soda, and pour it into a glass. He talks softly to her and lets her cry. At some point, I hear Farrah say in a strained voice, ". . . because you're Jewish . . ." My heart twists.

"Do you know her?" Mom asks Reuben, and he nods. "Who is she?"

Reuben moves us all into the living room, out of

Simon's earshot. "Her name is Farrah. She lives over by Uncle Sol's house."

"By *my* house?" my uncle says.

"Yeah, not too far from you."

"I've never seen her before," my uncle mutters.

"So, what does that mean, Sol? That she doesn't actually exist?" Mom says.

Uncle Sol turns away, mumbling under his breath. He lowers himself onto the couch, and Zeyde sits down next to him. Zeyde begins speaking to Uncle Sol in Yiddish, and I have no idea what they're saying.

Dad has a hand on Reuben's shoulder. I think he's about to ask Reuben some more questions about Farrah, but he whirls around toward the couch. "What did you just say, Sol?" My mom's family sometimes forgets that Dad speaks some Yiddish too.

"I said I'm never going to sell the hotel. The casinos will come and go, but the St. Bonaventure will always be on the Boardwalk." Uncle Sol crosses his arms over his chest.

Dad leans in like he didn't hear my uncle correctly. "Don't you listen to a single thing I tell you, Sol?" Uncle Sol turns red but doesn't say anything. "The writing is on the wall!" Dad continues. "The hotel will be bankrupt by the end of the year! I've told you a hundred times that you have to sell the place!"

Uncle Sol sinks farther down on the sofa cushion. Mom turns to him. "Sol?" Her voice is a plea and a warning.

Bankrupt? The St. Bonaventure? Dad's words hit me like bullets. I try to swallow. I try to breathe. I try to unhear what I just heard. But I can't.

So I run. Right out the front door. And I keep running.

We're all a bunch of liars. All of us. We're going under. We're drowning. We're weighed down by these secrets, these things we don't tell one another, and now I know things I wish I didn't know. And I'm no better than anyone else. I'm a fake too. I'm hiding things just like they are.

None of this, none of what happened today, is fair or right or just, or whatever word a person can use to describe something good. *God, I want to go up there and punch you right in the face. If you have a face. If you're up there.*

I have to stop running. I bend over, breathing heavily in the brutal heat, my hands on my knees. August should be outlawed.

When I look up, I can't believe where I am. I'm in front of Bubbe and Zeyde's synagogue. Afternoon light glimmers against the huge stained-glass window above the main doors. In the center of the window is a golden

Star of David, and in the center of the star, pieces of blue and white glass spell out one Hebrew word: *Emet*. Truth. The name of the synagogue is Beth Emet, House of Truth.

God sure has a strange sense of humor.

I lower myself to the sidewalk in front of the synagogue and cast my eyes down at my beat-up sneakers. Just one more week. I only have to lie to everyone for another week. I will not make things worse than they already are by spilling my guts to my family now. Besides, I get to spend the week with Melanie. Thinking about her brings some air back into my lungs.

I hadn't noticed before, but now I'm aware of people moving around me, families with kids, walking toward the synagogue. The little ones, some no more than preschool age, skip and hop inside, and their parents push strollers in behind them. Each time the doors open, music pours out onto the street—Jewish songs I've known since I was a preschooler myself. The familiar chords and the Hebrew words and the buzzing voices draw me in. A family with four little boys wearing matching blue kippot passes by me, and I follow them through the doors.

The lobby of the synagogue is packed. A huge yellow banner hangs from the ceiling: *Welcome, New Families!* Helium-filled balloons float over the crowd's heads, and kids are jumping as high as they can to try to grab the balloons' tails. Tables covered in brightly colored cloths overflow with cookies and cake. Children run around, chasing one another, while parents cluster together and chat. Music and laughter and kids' squeals surround me, and my shoulders relax for the first time all day.

"Hello, young man!" I turn to the voice coming at me from my left. A stout, bearded man in a dark blue suit reaches his hand out for me to shake. "You look lost. Where is your family? Are you new members?" A fancy Nikon camera hangs around his neck by a thick black leather strap.

"Oh, no," I say. "My grandparents are members, not me. I don't live around here."

"And who are your grandparents?" He hasn't let go of my hand yet, his grip firm and sure. He gazes at me like I'm the only other person in the room.

"The Broders," I reply.

The man's face lights up with recognition. "Of course! You're one of the boys!" He smiles and pats my shoulder. "You're one of the Goodman boys! I'm Rabbi Furman. I've known your grandparents for many years. You must be Joseph. Your bubbe and zeyde tell me all about your baseball games and your report cards!" I nod, but I'm not sure I've heard him right. Bubbe talks to the rabbi about me? *Me?*

A small, plump woman in a purple flowered dress catches the rabbi's arm. "Isaac, they want you in the classroom for the story time. You're supposed to read to the three-year-olds, remember?"

Rabbi Furman takes her elbow. "In a minute, dear." To me, he says, "This is my wife, Bernice. Bernie, this is Joseph Goodman, one of the Broders' grandsons."

Mrs. Furman claps her hands to her cheeks. "Oh! Joseph! Of course! Your bubbe talks about you all the time. Come, come." She removes the Nikon from around the rabbi's neck and holds it out to me. "You'll take pictures. My husband is not a photographer. He cuts off everyone's forehead when he takes pictures. You know how to use the camera? We need photos for the *Atlantic City Gazette*."

"You want *me* to take pictures?" I don't dare reach for the camera, so Mrs. Furman places the strap around my neck.

Mrs. Furman laughs. "Your bubbe says her boys can do anything! Here." She reaches into Rabbi Furman's jacket pocket. "Here's another roll of film, in case you need it. Now, the rabbi must go read to the children." Rabbi Furman bows his head to me, and they move toward a hallway leading off the lobby.

I can't believe it! I take the Nikon in my hands and hold it like it's a huge, delicate egg. It's perfect.

I have no idea how to use this thing. But I'm going to figure it out. Could a photograph that I take end up in the newspaper?

The crowd in the lobby spreads out as people make their way down various hallways to other parts of the building. I haven't moved since shaking the rabbi's hand. I roll my neck back and forth and switch the camera on. When I raise the viewfinder to my face, it's like opening my eyes for the first time.

I glide around the lobby, my eye against the clear square of the viewfinder, and stories unfold to me. A kid on tiptoes reaches for a cookie on a tabletop, and I press the shutter just as he turns his head to see if his mother is looking. A father holds a sleeping baby with a tiny knitted kippah against his shoulder. I capture that too. When a teenager begins to lead a game of Hebrew Simon Says, I snap a photo of a pack of children with their hands on their ears.

I stride down a hallway and enter the classroom where Rabbi Furman is reading to a circle of kids sitting cross-legged on the carpeted floor. The rabbi is sitting in a chair meant for someone a quarter of his size, and he's taken his jacket off and rolled up his shirtsleeves. He holds up a page that shows an illustration of a huge tree with a thousand branches.

"This is the Tree of Life," Rabbi Furman says, his voice filled with wonder.

A toddler points and yells, "Twee!" The adults standing outside the circle laugh. So does the rabbi.

"Yes! Very good! It *is* a tree! It is the happiest tree in the world, and anyone who holds on to it will be happy and peaceful." I take a photo of the rabbi's face as he says this. His blue eyes shimmer in the classroom's fluorescent light.

Rabbi Furman begins to sing "Eytz Chaim, Tree of Life," a song whose notes are as familiar to me as "Happy Birthday." Voices join in, and in a moment, I realize that I'm singing too. The words, the music, fill the room and fill me, and maybe this is what it's like to know that God is here. I'm part of something here, part of something I've known all my life. We sing about the Torah and learning and renewal. The rabbi's eyes meet mine, and he nods to me as our voices carry across the room.

A hand touches my shoulder, and a strong voice sounds near my ear. When I look behind me, my father is there, smiling and singing with all of us. He wears a black kippah, and he places one on my head too. When the song ends, the children clap and beg Rabbi Furman for another. Dad pulls me into the hallway.

"How did you know I was here?" I ask.

"Rabbi Furman's wife called Bubbe's house. She said you'd come in. She was worried because you were here by yourself." He points to the Nikon. "Are you the syna-gogue photographer now?"

I launch into the story of my afternoon, and Dad bobs his head, impressed.

"Can I stay a little while longer?" I ask. "I have a whole other roll of film I can take."

"If you'd like. I'll be your assistant. What do I need to do?"

We stay for another hour or so, until I finish both rolls of film. I teach myself how to focus the lens and wind the film. The event is still in full swing when I return the camera and film to Mrs. Furman. "Thank you so much," I say as I hand the Nikon over to her.

"You enjoyed the afternoon?" she asks.

I nod and pull my shoulders up. "I loved it. Every-thing about it."

Dad and I make our way back to my grandparents' house. I don't know what to expect when I get there. We walk side by side, and Dad drapes his arm around my shoulder.

The sun moves across the summer sky, and the heat, which felt so oppressive earlier, settles around me now like something comforting and welcome.

Tomorrow I'm going to tell Artie that I don't want to work for him anymore, that I'm done. I'm done lying, and I'm done worrying myself sick about Ralphie and Grunts and Cadillacs and stolen TVs. I'll just walk away from them.

But . . .

But if I do that, I'll never see Melanie again.

And even though I'm upset that she gave Reuben her phone number, I still want to see her. I can't walk away from *her*. Maybe I should stick with it for the week.

Anyway, a person can't just quit a job halfway through, right?

I think about this all the way back to the house. When Dad and I step through the door, the place is as still as a painting.

Most of the adults are napping in various chairs and on sofas. Reuben and Mom are in the kitchen. She's serving him a plate of cold chicken and sliced tomatoes. I don't see Simon, so he must have gone somewhere with Farrah, or something. In the laundry room, Ben is sitting on the floor, making a clown face on his Lite-Brite. A large black-and-blue mark stains his arm where it hit the table earlier. He looks up at me when I come into the room. I know he's a good actor and all, but his brown eyes are huge and round and miserable, and I know he's not faking it. When I left before, I left Ben all alone, even in this house full of people.

"Hey, Beans," I say, and my voice sounds far away, even to me. "Want to play a game?"

Ben nods. He pulls the colored pegs out of the Lite-Brite board and places them in the box while I go to the cabinet and look over the games stored there. "Want to play Kerplunk?"

"No, that's too noisy. Let's play Sorry."

"Sorry it is." I smile down at him, and he smiles back. Even though that smile doesn't reach his eyes, at least I'm not making things worse.

CHAPTER 9

No one speaks on the ride to the hotel on Monday. Mom lets Reuben drive, and she sits in the passenger seat with her head back and her eyes closed. Simon chews on his thumbnail and stares out the window. Ben leans on me and examines his bruised arm. It feels like it's been weeks since I last saw Melanie, not just three days. I don't know how much I want to tell her about the weekend or if she even wants to hear it. But I do want to ask Artie why Ralphie drove by my grandparents' house like he was casing it out.

Even the hotel seems somber this morning. The lobby is empty, and the only sound comes from the water bubbling out of the frogs' mouths in the fountain.

"Do you want to go to the beach after breakfast?" Mom asks Ben as she tousles his hair.

Ben shrugs. "Maybe the pool."

"Okay, honey." I've never seen her looking more like Bubbe. She's aged ten years in the past two weeks. She must be worried about the hotel too.

I turn away and try to think about something else, anything else.

Like what Melanie and I are going to do this week. We did everything last week that I can imagine us doing.

Well, not everything.

I know what I want to do. And I think Melanie will be impressed.

★ ★ ★

"Really?" she says when I pick her up. "Like, really?"

"Yeah! Let's go see the ape woman."

We amble down the Boardwalk, and Melanie spins around me, her hair whipping in the hot breeze, her smile electric. She's wearing a red sundress with tiny polka dots scattered across the skirt and a pair of bright white Keds. The sneakers make her look younger, more like a kid. "This is going to be amazing, Goodman!" she shouts into the wind.

The drums beat in my head as soon as we step onto Million Dollar Pier. I will not be afraid of this ridiculous sham of a show. I refuse to be.

We're the first people in line. We stand in front of the building's entryway, a wooden door that's been scraped and scratched up to look like, I don't know, a door in the jungle? It's not like I expected an accurate recreation of an ape's natural habitat, but I still can't help cringing. Melanie presses her ear to the door, so I do the same. Those drums will be booming when we go inside.

"Get back, kids!"

We jump away, and a man with white hair and a short white beard stretches his body across the door. He's wearing what I guess is supposed to be a safari outfit: a tan, short-sleeved, button-down shirt and those shorts with a hundred pockets. He also has on a pith helmet and heavy boots. I'm sweating buckets just looking at him. "You shouldn't go in there!" he cries. "The ape woman will tear you apart!" He covers his mouth with the back of his hand, like he can't even talk about it anymore.

Melanie rolls her eyes at me. "If that happens, will you refund the entry fee?" I crack up, but our laughter doesn't faze Safari Man.

"Laugh if you want," he says, and he leans in close to us. He makes his eyebrows roll over his eyes like furry centipedes. "The ape woman has broken free of her shackles before!"

My heart is ticking away, but I keep up a cool front. "Well, it's our lives!" I say. "Let us in!"

Safari Man scratches his cheek. "We usually wait for a few more people before we open the doors." He steps back and goes into character again. "Who wants to see the ape woman? She transforms before your eyes!"

We wait and wait. I think I'm too sweaty and sluggish to be afraid at this point. It must be twenty after by the time a "crowd" gathers, and that's only eight or nine people. A family with triplet girls who look to be about Ben's age lines up right behind us. The dad stares at the sky, and the mother takes out a compact and applies bright red lipstick while the girls swat at each other and whine about the heat. The crown of my head is sizzling by the time Safari Man starts his preshow speech. He rattles on about not approaching the stage inside and how the strobe lights may affect pregnant women.

"Don't look at me!" the triplets' mother says when we all do. "You want ape women? Come to our house around nine o'clock at night!" The girls giggle, and the dad sighs.

Just as Safari Man warns us again that we're taking our lives in our hands, the door swings open. At this point, the air-conditioning feels so good that I forget why I was scared in the first place. We walk down a short hallway lined with fake trees with hanging vines and enormous plastic leaves. Music that I'm guessing is supposed to sound mysterious blares from loudspeakers on the walls. Melanie squeezes my arm. "I'm so excited!" she says in my ear, and I laugh. I'm glad it's dark because I know I'm blushing.

The space opens up at the end of the hallway, and now we stand before a small, dark stage. A large piece of fabric painted to look like the inside of a tent drapes the wall at the back of the stage. A smoke machine hisses to our left, coughing feeble puffs of white fog around our legs. The last person enters the room, and a door shuts tight behind him. I'm no longer afraid of the ape woman, but I really hope a fire doesn't break out in here. The room is a death trap.

The whole show lasts five minutes, tops. Safari Man's recorded voice narrates a silly story, and a woman in a loincloth and a bikini top, who looks like Jane from the Tarzan movies, is pushed out onto the stage in a cage.

"Well, that's creepy," Melanie mutters. She's right. The woman slinks around the cage, and she's selling her part pretty well. After we're blinded by strobe lights and choked by fake smoke, and after we pretend not to see the projector strategically placed in the jungle foliage, a very fake ape seems to have replaced the woman in the cage. It beats its chest and howls. After a moment its whole body slackens and it goes totally quiet. The jungle sounds fall off, and I figure that's the end of the show.

But it's not. The ape raises its head and wails again. It rattles the bars of the cage, and the whole thing starts to sway. My pulse starts racing, and I clench my jaw so tight that I think it's going to break off.

The strobe and all the other lights cut out, and the ape noises multiply. In the pitch blackness, all three of the triplets scream. Melanie grips my arm and draws in her breath.

A screeching, furry, glow-in-the-dark shape appears before us and leaps from the stage. The people on the floor draw back, stunned, as the glowing ape raises its arms over its head, bellows, and runs out of the room to our left.

The lights come up, and Melanie doubles over giggling. The triplets cry and yell, while others press their hands to their faces and stomachs and let out moans of relief. Now that the show is over, the tension whooshes out of me and I shake with laughter.

The door behind us opens, and we walk back down the hallway toward the entrance. Safari Man shakes our hands and congratulates us on surviving the wrath of the ape woman. He pushes open the door to the pier, and sunlight floods in. We blink at the light like bears coming out of hibernation. My eyes water, and I'm dying for something to drink. I lead Melanie to a refreshment stand and order us Cokes. We sit on a bench in front of a kiddie ride. Three- and four-year-olds sit in candy-colored miniature cars, going around and around in a slow circle.

"That was messed up," I say.

Melanie nods slowly. "Very messed up." We listen to the amusement park music and watch the little kids squeeze the car horns and pretend to drive. Neither of us speaks for a while.

Finally, Melanie says, "I'll bet Eddie looks a lot like that ape when he gets up in the morning," and we laugh so hard my stomach hurts.

★　★　★

When we arrive back at Pinky's, Eddie's standing outside. He has tugged his tie open to give himself a little breathing room, but he's panting hard in the heat. He holds a bottle of Dr. Pepper in one hand and a folded-up section of the newspaper in the other. I've only known Eddie for two weeks now, but I know he's not reading about the latest crisis in the Middle East. He's running down the lineups for the horse races at Garden State Park.

"Look who it is," Melanie says. "Eddie, what are you waiting out here for? You look like you're suffocating in that outfit."

Eddie shifts his weight from one foot to the other and back. He's in a black suit, and he looks like a sweaty waiter. "I'm not waiting for you, little girl. Just go inside, will ya? You're blocking my view." Melanie laughs and opens the door. As I pass by him, Eddie says, "Good-man, when are you gonna give me a shot to win my money back, huh?" He smirks, pats me on the shoulder, and adds, "Rotten kid."

I smile at him. "See ya, Eddie." I let the door close behind me. That guy has really grown on me.

The arcade is hopping, wall-to-wall teenagers playing pinball and Skee-Ball and standing in clumps flirting with one another. I straighten up and ease my way through the crowd, a relaxed grin on my face. I'm glad I didn't quit this job, no matter how good it felt to be at synagogue. I'm starting to think that Ralphie driving by my grandparents' house over the weekend was just a coincidence. What could he possibly want with me? I'm one of Artie's guys too.

In the back, Melanie takes a seat on a stool at the bar, and Tommy pours her a glass of iced tea. "You want one, Good-man?" Tommy calls out when he sees me.

"Sure, I'll be right there," I reply, and I wave to Artie.

He wears the same suit he wore the first day we met in the diner. The red tie is a perfect knot at his throat. He sees me and signals toward the back door, like he wants me to go out there. He looks so serious. I rack my brain, trying to think if I've done something wrong.

I step out back. Ralphie leans on a railing by a set of steps leading down to a sidewalk. He smokes a cigarette and mops his forehead with a handkerchief. *Okay, what's going on?*

A hand falls on my shoulder, and Artie is next to me. "Joey, come take a walk with me."

He leads me toward the steps. I swallow hard. I don't have much choice but to go with him. Ralphie tosses his cigarette when he sees us approach. Blood pulses in my temples so loudly that I'm sure Artie can hear it.

"Good-man, how you doin'?" Ralphie says. From his grim expression, I know he doesn't want an answer.

Artie grips my shoulder tighter. "Joey, I need you to do something for me." He moves in front of me and locks his eyes with mine.

"What?" It's the only word I can form.

"Your family, they're all at the hotel right now, right? Not at your grandparents' house?"

I lick my lips and shake my head. "No, they're not at the house."

"You sure?" Artie asks.

Why does he need to know?

"They're not at the house." It comes out like I'm asking him.

"Okay, good. So, Joey, we're friends, right? Good friends?"

Something curdles in my stomach. "Yeah."

"Sure we are," he says. "We're practically family. And people in families do favors for each other sometimes, right? Well, I need you to do me a favor today, Joey. Ralphie here is going to drive you to your grandparents' house. In the car, he's got a package. I need you to hide that package for me. Not for long, just for a couple of days."

I swallow, and my spit feels like fire going down. "What kind of package?"

"Just a small package," Artie says. "Now, you're not going to look in the package, and you're not going to tell anyone about it, understand? Not your parents, not your brothers, nobody. Deal?"

"I . . . I don't know. I need to think about it." I glance at Ralphie, but Artie takes my chin in his hand and turns my face back toward him.

"You can do this, Joey," he says. "I have faith in you, remember? You're strong! You're one of my boys."

I open and close my mouth. Twice. I'm taking too long to respond.

I could say no.

No, I can't. I can't say no to the king of Steel Pier.

"Okay."

Artie pats my head like I'm a puppy. "Terrific, kiddo. Ralphie's going to bring you over there now. Your grandparents have a storage room that's full of junk, right?"

Did I tell him that? I did, didn't I? "Yeah, but—"

"That's where you can hide the package," Artie says. "With the junk. It'll blend right in." My mind spins. Should I tell him what happened the last time I hid something in that storage room?

Doing this means lying to my family. Again. I knead my hands together like I'm trying to break my own fingers.

But I can make this work. I can. I won't make the same mistake twice. There are a hundred places in that storage room where I could hide a small package. I nod at Artie, then at Ralphie. "Sure."

Artie backs away a step. "All right, so you go do that now, and Ralphie will drive you back to the St. Bonaventure. And you'll keep this just between us." He gestures at each of us, and without another word, he walks back toward Pinky's.

"Car's over here, kid," Ralphie says, and he points away from the Boardwalk, toward the road into town. He lumbers sideways down the steps and grunts when he reaches the bottom. I follow him on the sidewalk, and we pass some old brick houses and a motel. My palms may as well be dripping, they're so sweaty. What would Ralphie do if I just took off down the street right now?

I assume he's leading me to the white Cadillac, but when he finally stops about four blocks from the

Boardwalk, he slides a key in the lock of a gold Ford sedan with a black vinyl roof. Ralphie settles himself behind the wheel and leans over to unlock my door. I slide in, and the cloth seat is like a scratchy, hot towel against my thighs.

Ralphie huffs and pants a bit as he turns on the car and rolls down his window. "No air-conditioning in this thing, Good-man. You'd better roll that window down."

I glance around the inside of the car, wondering where this package is. Maybe it's in the trunk. If this is Ralphie's car, maybe it wasn't even Ralphie in that Caddy that passed by the house the other day. Maybe it was some other guy who just looked similar to Ralphie.

"You're over in Margate, right?" he asks as we start off. He doesn't wait for an answer and turns down Atlantic Avenue.

"Yeah, Kenyon Avenue, near the—" I almost say it's near the Jewish community center, but that's probably not a landmark on Ralphie's radar.

"Sure, sure. I know where you mean."

I chew my lip. Of course he doesn't need directions. He knows where he's going.

The stink of cigarette and cigar smoke clings to every surface. I stick my head out the window to try to gulp in some fresh air.

He turns on the radio and plays with the channel knob until he hears Tony Bennett. "You like Tony?"

"I don't really listen to him."

"No? What do you listen to? Sinatra? Sammy Davis?"

"No, I like rock music."

Ralphie makes a *pfft* sound. "Rock music? That stuff is junk! You can't even understand the words!"

"You can understand the Beatles."

He snorts. "Them Beatles ain't even American! Don't you listen to any American music?"

"Sure. I like the Beach Boys. They're American."

He stops at a red light and turns to me. "Listen, Good-man. If you're not gonna listen to Frank or Tony, at least listen to Ray Charles or Sam Cooke. Now that's music."

"My dad loves Ray Charles," I say. "He listens to that one album all the time." Does Ralphie really need to know what music my father likes? I wipe drops of sweat from my temple.

The light turns green, and he nods a couple of times as he pulls away. "Sammy Davis Jr. is a Jew, y'know."

"Is he?" I'm not really interested in the answer. Artie was so right—Ralphie does talk too much.

But he's not done. "Jews are smart. Very tough, but smart people. You know what I mean. Gotta be careful because they're always trying to pull a fast one on you." I close my eyes and lean my cheek against the car door. "My sister's kid married a Jew, and he's real smart. He's a big-time dentist in New York. Spiegel, Jerry Spiegel. You know him?"

I swallow, trying to clear the sour taste in my mouth. "We don't all know each other," I say.

Ralphie doesn't respond, and I know he's not listening to me at all. My shoulders tighten so hard they could crack walnuts.

We're getting close to Bubbe's house. I don't want to talk anymore. I want to get this over with and get back to the St. Bonaventure. If I could jump out of this car right now, I would.

Ralphie doesn't even pretend not to know which house is the right one. He pulls up in front, but before he turns the car off, he asks, "There's a driveway in the back, right?" He knows that answer too, so he pulls the car around to the back of the house and into the driveway. He kills the engine and twists toward me in his seat. "You remember what Artie said, right? You don't tell nobody about this." I nod.

He reaches over to my side and opens the glove compartment. He takes out a small, rectangular package wrapped in rough, gray paper and a ton of black tape. I couldn't open it even if I wanted to, which I do not. He's not handling it delicately, so it's probably not some kind of bomb. The *thud-thud-thud* in my ears dulls a bit.

Ralphie leans back in his seat and holds up the

package. "Here it is, kid. Now, come on, let's go find a place for it."

Wait, what? As in the two of us *together*? "You don't have to come in!" I say, maybe a little too quickly. "I can find a good place. I know just the spot, actually."

He lets his arm fall into his lap. "Good-man, you didn't think I was gonna let you go in by yourself, did you? You're a good kid and everything, but I don't trust nobody." He pushes his door open and spills out onto the driveway.

I stare at the glove box for a minute. I brought this goon to my house. I started this. Now, I have to finish it.

CHAPTER 10

No one's around, so I'm not too concerned about sneaking Ralphie into the house. He's not someone who can be snuck in somewhere anyway. As always, the back door is unlocked. We enter through the laundry room. The AC coats me, and I need it because I'm sweating for several different reasons at this point. I've never thought about how the inside of the house looks to someone who's never seen it before. The laundry room has those stacks of old papers on the floor, and Mom's underwear is draped over a string hanging above the washer and dryer. I pray that Ralphie doesn't turn his head. Or that if he does, he doesn't say anything creepy.

But Ralphie's all business right now. "Where's that storage room?" he asks. I lead him through the kitchen, where my grandmother cooks her matzo ball soup, and through the dining room, where my family has Passover seders, to the double doors of the storage room.

Ralphie's eyes wander over the wide doorframe. "This used to be the garage, I take it."

"Yeah. They made that driveway out back when

they converted this to storage." I pull open the door on the right and take a deep breath before moving into the dark room. I flip on the light, and Ralphie looks around, taking it all in.

He nods a few times. "This is perfect. Okay, avoid anything at eye level. We have to find a space either on the floor, hidden by stuff, or way up high on those shelves."

I step around what I have to, trying not to topple the encyclopedia set like dominoes. Ralphie stays in his spot just inside the door. He's not exactly the ideal size for tiptoeing. I make my way over to a corner jammed with stacks of old St. Bonaventure dishes. "What about here? Behind all these?"

Ralphie shakes his head. "No, gotta be someplace that's completely out of sight. You might be able to see into that corner from another angle."

This is taking too long. What if my mother and Ben come back to the house to get showered here before dinner? What if Simon decides he's not working the dinner shift and he ends up back here? We have to find a place to hide this package now. My eyes dart over every inch of the room, but no place seems safe enough.

Until . . .

"I got it!" I say, and I scuttle over to the shelves on the opposite wall. I stand on my tiptoes, and from the shelf just within reach, I grab a blue vinyl case with a black plastic handle. A large sticker on the front says HOT WHEELS in red and yellow letters with flames coming off them. When I bring it down, the few cars that are in the case make a jangling sound like a janitor shaking a huge key ring. Ralphie scowls at me, and I freeze. But after a second, I puff out a breath. *Get this over with, Joey!*

Ralphie hands me the package. It's heavy as a brick. I put the Hot Wheels case on a lower shelf and open it. There are a bunch of little cars in the case, but there's plenty of room for the package. I push the cars over to one side and place the package in with them. My eye catches one car: a red 1963 Corvette Stingray. It was my favorite Hot Wheels car. Dad bought it for me for my ninth birthday, and I never let anyone touch it, not even Reuben. I remember telling Dad that I'd drive that car someday and that the only person I'd allow in the car was Mom because she made the best PB&Js. The memory jars me.

"Hey, let's go!" Ralphie says through gritted teeth. I pocket the Corvette, and then I close and lock the case.

We're back in the Ford in no time.

"That was good, kid," Ralphie says. "You did good." I force a thin smile, but Ralphie's not looking at me.

I sag into the seat and let out a huff of relief that it's over—for now, anyway. I don't know how I'm going to live in that house, knowing that package is there, knowing I've just done something possibly illegal and probably dangerous. I don't know how many more things I can hide from my family. My stomach clenches like I've taken a body blow from Muhammad Ali.

* * *

Tonight, Reuben and Simon disappear out the door as soon as we get back to the house after dinner. It's just me and Mom and Ben. Ben has been quiet today—so unlike him—but Mom has been too. What if she knew what I was doing behind her back, behind everyone's backs? It would hurt her—*I* would hurt her—if she found out about Melanie and Artie and Ralphie and the package and the money and . . .

This will all be over soon. I only have four more days with Melanie, with Artie. Because, really, once this week is up and Mel goes back to Hackensack, Artie won't need me around anymore. And the package will be—well, wherever it will be as long as it's not here. And that means I'll go back to being just Joey again.

If I can. That Joey may be long gone.

I want to go back in time to yesterday, when Dad and I were together in Beth Emet, when I lifted that camera to my eye, when I felt sure about where I belong and who I am. Yesterday, I didn't just know that I was part of something; I knew I was meant for something.

But that was yesterday.

I'm dead asleep by the time Reuben and Simon come home. I don't even hear them come in.

★ ★ ★

When Mel and I get outside on Tuesday, thunder rumbles. Rain threatens to pour down on us any minute now, one of those warm rains with huge droplets that snap against your skin like bee stings. Melanie and I start down the boards.

"Hey," she says, "let's take a ride on one of those cart things that they push down the Boardwalk. You know? The pushcarts?"

"You mean the rolling chairs? They're expensive."

She leans in close and grabs my arm. She smells like cocoa butter. "Eddie gave me twenty bucks just now. Can you believe that? Twenty bucks!"

I don't really want to do this. Riding a rolling chair is embarrassing. But I can see how much she wants to go, so I say, "Fine, let's go get a ride."

The rolling chairs are a classic Boardwalk attraction. For the tourists, that is. People from Atlantic City never ride them. They're cushioned benches covered by large canopies, kind of like a rolling version of a window seat. They look fun because you sit there and someone pushes you down the Boardwalk. But it's not like you're being pushed so fast that it's exciting or anything. The drivers don't jog down the Boardwalk. It's like taking a car to go visit a friend who lives down the street.

But I'm not about to say any of this to Melanie. The bench seats on the rolling chairs aren't that big, and I'm running scenarios in my head to calculate how close we could end up sitting to each other.

We have to walk a while before we see any chairs. They're not all over the Boardwalk like they used to be. We finally spot three empty ones lined up along the railing overlooking the beach. The three drivers perch atop the railing, their shoulders hunched, like buzzards on a branch. They're college boys whose cheerless faces tell me they'd much rather be poolside right about now.

Melanie does the talking when we approach them. "Hey, can we get a ride in one of these?"

The blond guy on the end shakes his hair back from his face and jumps down from the railing. "Rides aren't free, you know. They cost money."

Melanie shrugs. "We have money."

The guy next to the blonde smiles lazily. I want to smack the grin off his face. He's got patchy sideburns, like he can't grow them fully.

Blondie folds his arm across his chest. "Ten bucks for ten minutes."

"Seriously?" Melanie says. "That's ridiculous!"

Sideburns hops down from the railing and gyrates his hips toward Melanie. "I'll let you ride for free, if you lose your little friend." He laughs, and the idiot who's still on the railing joins in.

I take a step forward and ball my hands into fists. "Don't talk to her like that!"

Sideburns sidles up to me. His threadbare Grateful Dead T-shirt hangs limp on his bony shoulders. "Who are you, her mother?"

Melanie takes hold of my left arm and tries to pull me away. "Come on, Joey. Let's just go."

"Yeah, *Joey*, run along!" Sideburns pushes my shoulder, and I stumble back.

Rage rushes through me like a storm, and I shove him with both hands as hard as I can.

Sideburns rocks back, and his mouth falls open. He narrows his eyes at me. "You're in a world of trouble now!" He lunges for me, but the blond guy holds him back.

"Let him go, man! He's just a kid. You wanna get fired?"

Sideburns snarls and strains against his pal's arms. My breath comes fast and shallow through my nose.

"Joey! Come on!" Melanie grabs my shirt and pulls me away. We turn and bolt down the Boardwalk. We're blocks away before Sideburns's shouts and threats fade in my ears.

I want to keep running, but a huge lump sinks in my stomach like a stone. I stop and bend forward, my arms wrapped around my middle. *What did I just do?* My chin trembles, and something dark and heavy fills me up.

Artie's face flashes across my mind. He would've wanted me to shove that guy, or even fight him. That's what King Artie expects of his people. Might before right. Is that who I am now?

Artie asks me to come out back again when we arrive at Pinky's. I don't have the strength to protest, so I follow him through the back door. Rain still threatens, and the humidity is killer. Clouds like soaked cotton press the sky downward until the air is a solid wall against my face. Breathing takes a lot of effort.

He puts his hand on my shoulder. "Ralphie said you hid the package real good for me."

I raise my eyes to his. "It's only going to be a couple of days, right?"

Artie nods. "Sure, sure. Only a few days. Absolutely."

I've been lying so much these days that I can even tell when someone is lying to me.

★　★　★

The Hot Wheels Corvette sits on the squat table next to my cot at the house. Despite a weariness that has dug its way down into my bones, I can't sleep, so I lie on my side and push the little car back and forth across the table. I remember thinking that Hot Wheels cars were life's greatest invention when I was younger. This Corvette looks so small now. How did they even put the flame decals on something so tiny?

A noise from downstairs startles me. Reuben and Simon went out again tonight, so it must be them coming home. Their voices float up the stairs, but I can't make out what they're saying. Things have been weird between Reuben and me since we had that argument on the Boardwalk. We're not avoiding each other, exactly, but we're not actually talking either.

I tense up when I hear one of them coming up the steps. It's Reuben. I know the sounds that everyone in this house makes.

When he walks by my room without knocking to come in, my chest tightens. I roll onto my back. No, I'm not sorry for what I said to him the other day, but can't he just come talk to me? Can't he at least say good night?

After Reuben closes the door to his and Simon's bedroom, I wait for Simon to come upstairs. I want to ask him how Farrah is, if she's okay. Simon has been super quiet for the past few days too. Reuben seems to be the only person he talks to.

But Simon doesn't come up the steps. I wait and wait for what must be half an hour. I don't even hear any sounds from downstairs anymore. No TV, no cabinets opening and closing in the kitchen. Maybe he fell asleep on the couch.

I bolt upright.

Maybe he's in the storage room.

Maybe he went in there to get an ice cream or something, and maybe he noticed that things weren't in exactly the same spots they'd always been. Maybe I didn't put the Hot Wheels case back on the shelf the same way I got it down. Maybe he's already found—

I dash out of the bedroom and down the stairs. I try the living room first, hoping I'll find Simon sleeping. But he's not there. I move from room to room. No Simon. I press my lips together so hard my teeth may go right through them as I steal toward the dining room. I hear faint sounds now.

Light from inside the storage room bleeds into the dining room. Simon is in there. Panic burns through me like a trail of gasoline that's just been lit. *Oh, God, please keep that package hidden!* I tiptoe into the dining room. More noise from the storage room. Simon is moving things around. Why is he moving things around in the middle of the night? I edge past the dining room table and over to the storage room entrance.

Simon and I nearly bump into each other in the doorway. I let out a cry and flinch. Simon jumps back. "What the heck, squirt!"

"I-I heard noises down here." He's blocking the doorway, and I can't see inside the storage room. I try to look around him. "What were you doing in there?"

Simon forces me backward and comes out of the room. "Nothing," he says, and he shuts the door behind him.

His hands are empty. So there's that, at least. I whirl around and head back toward the kitchen. Simon follows on my tail. I look around the kitchen like I'm thinking of buying the place.

"It's time for bed, squirt. Let's go." He gestures toward the stairway.

We stare at each other for a moment. "Right," I say.

Simon is on my heels going up the steps. As soon as I'm in my room with the door closed, I dig myself under the covers like a mole tunneling under the dirt. But I won't be able to sleep.

CHAPTER 11

In the chaos of everyone trying to get out of the house this morning, I didn't have a chance to go into the storage room and check for Artie's package. I'm kicking myself because I should have done it last night, after Simon went to bed, but I was too upset from running into him. I can't believe I still let Simon have that effect on me. My temples pound, like someone is kneading wet sand in my ears, so I fold forward and close my eyes as we drive to the hotel. I'll go straight to the storage room when we get home tonight.

At breakfast, I follow Reuben around and try to do my usual. But I knock over Mrs. Birnbaum's water (she gives very scary stink eye), and I sneeze directly on a bread basket in front of a table of guests. At one point, I actually fall. I outright trip over my own feet and land facedown in a pile of cracker crumbs on the floor next to Mr. Levy's orthopedic shoes.

"What are you doing down there, young man?" he asks. It takes me a few seconds to get over my complete humiliation and start to scramble to my feet.

"Sorry, sir," Reuben says as he lifts me under my armpit and pulls me over to the nearest waiter's stand. He grips my arm and says, "Why don't you just leave a little early today, huh, Joey? You're going to go meet up with Melanie, right? Just go ahead. Go now."

I yank my arm away. "You're not Dad, you know. And you're not Bubbe. You can't tell me what to do." Some guests at a nearby table frown at us.

Reuben brings his face close to mine. "Stop it, Joey. Right now, in this room, I'm your boss, and I'm telling you to take the rest of the shift off."

I glower at him. "Fine. See you later, *boss*." I stalk out of the room, passing Bubbe, whose arms are folded across her chest like a prison warden.

God forbid anyone should make a scene in this half-full dining room with its hideous, fifty-year-old wall-paper and ancient, splintery tables.

I change my clothes and grumble at Uncle Sol when he asks what's wrong as I trample through the lobby. I frown at the ugly ceramic frogs in the fountain. I think I hate those frogs. I yank my kippah off my head and toss it onto a table near the revolving door.

Everything is wrong now. Everything except Melanie. The heat and humidity that smack me as I step onto the Boardwalk only prove my point. I look around, and everyone on the boards wears a sour expression, a pinched mouth, narrow eyes. No one is happy to be in Atlantic City anymore.

Even though it's only nine o'clock, I decide to go to Pinky's now. I don't have my bag of tickets or my money with me, but I find a mangled dollar bill in my pocket that must have gone through the wash with my shorts. I want to play some Skee-Ball and get my mind off . . . well, everything.

Pinky's is basically empty, but I do see Ralphie and Grunts at a table in the back. Their heads are close together, and Grunts is hanging on Ralphie's every word. Ralphie draws on the table with his finger and points to a couple of spots. Grunts nods a lot. It's like Ralphie is suddenly the most fascinating teacher in the world. Ralphie is planning something. I know it. Or maybe I'm seeing something that's not there. But Ralphie's eyes sure are taking on an icy look more and more.

I get my quarters and head to the Skee-Ball machines without saying hello to anyone in the back. In what seems like the blink of an eye, I only have four balls left in my last game. I'm concentrating so hard on Skee-Ball that I don't notice Melanie come up beside me. She knocks me with her hip and says, "Get out of my way, Goodman. Those last four are mine!"

"Hey, I paid for this game!" I say, and I lift an index finger in the air and pretend to call out to the guy at the prize table. "Sir? Sir, this person is bothering me!"

Melanie giggles and lines up her roll. She brings her arm back and then flings it forward. The ball flies through the air like a baseball and slams into the backboard with a sharp crack. It bounces off and comes rolling back down the alley toward us. I laugh.

"Wow, that was bad," Melanie says. "I don't know my own strength!" She drops the ball in my hand. "Here, you play. I'm going to get some money from my dad for us." When she comes back, I'm down to my last ball. I want to show off a little in front of her, so I let the ball fly, and it jumps into the fifty-point hole like a baby kangaroo bounding into its mother's pouch. Melanie claps.

"Wow! Look at all those!" She points to the tickets gathering on the floor as the machine spits them out.

I fold them up and present them to her like the prince presenting the glass slipper to Cinderella. "You may have them," I say. "You can go get a bouncy ball or something from the prize table."

Melanie drops her jaw and puts her hands to her chest. "Really? Oh, Goodman, you know how to win a girl over." She trots off to the prize table and comes back with a pink plastic ring on her index finger. She puts her hand up next to her cheek. "For my huge jewelry collection," she says in a terrible French accent. "Let's get out of here. I don't want to be inside all day."

On the Boardwalk, she nudges me with her elbow. "It's Wednesday, Goodman. Three days left until I head home. Two, if you don't count today."

"I'm counting today." How can I not count today?

We stroll for a bit, directionless, and Melanie tells me about her school up in Hackensack. She goes to a huge public school, and she hopes she gets Mrs. O'Hara for English this year.

"This is my last year at my school," I say. "I've always gone to the Jewish day school. But after eighth grade, my parents are forcing me to go to public high school against my will."

She nods. "I know. Reuben told me. That's awful!"

What? I stop in the middle of the Boardwalk. "When did you talk to Reuben?"

"When we were out last night."

I couldn't have heard that right. "You were out last night. With Reuben."

"Yes. Wait, you didn't know?"

"Didn't know?" As if repeating her words is going to change them.

Melanie holds her palms up, like it's obvious. "That Reuben and I have gone out a couple times."

"A *couple* times?"

"Yeah. Saturday night. Monday night. Last night. I thought Reuben would've mentioned it."

My chest hurts. "You're not supposed to go out with Reuben!"

Melanie jerks her head back. "I'm not *supposed* to? How is who I go out with any of your business?"

My shock gives way to something darker. "He's got a real girlfriend at home. He's just wasting time with you."

She flinches. "Stop it, Joey."

But I can't stop it now. "You went out with him behind my back because you know it's wrong. I thought we were friends. How could you have lied to me?"

"Oh, and you're asking me this because you're such a model of honesty?" A vein in her forehead throbs. "You lie to your family every day when you leave the hotel."

My face burns because I know she's right. For a moment I don't know what to say. I end up blurting out, "Reuben's using you."

It should be her eyes that are filling up right now, not mine.

"Did it ever occur to you, Goodman, that maybe *I'm* using *him*? That maybe we're using each other? Just to have a little fun before we both leave this crummy city?" She storms off but only goes a few steps before she spins around and stomps back to me. She holds her index finger an inch from my nose. "You know what? You're fired. I don't need you following me around for the next three days." She digs in the pocket of her shorts and comes up with two ten-dollar bills, which she stuffs in my hand. "Here's what we owe you." This time when she walks off, she keeps going.

I gaze at the crumpled bills in my open palm and let the breeze sweep them off my hand and onto the boards. A little girl walking by stomps on them, first one and then the other, to hold them down. She picks them up from beneath her sandals and examines them. Her eyes meet mine for a moment before she runs off, yelling, "Daddy! Daddy! Look what I found! It's money!"

I dig the heels of my hands into my eyes. When I look down the Boardwalk again, I can still see Melanie—her long, black ponytail bouncing against her back as she moves away from me.

"Melanie!" I yell as the last speck of her dissolves in the distance. "Melanie!" People on the Boardwalk are eyeing me. They move around me like my misery is contagious. I ride out a wave of pain in my belly until I can stand straight again.

This cannot be how this ends.

★ ★ ★

"I need to work the lunch shift," I say to Bubbe when I get back to the kitchen at the St. Bonaventure. I want to add *just not with Reuben*, but I don't. I'm not about to explain this situation to my grandmother. My jumpiness from earlier has been replaced by a grim twist to my mouth.

"Not with that face," she replies. She returns to unpacking a box of jelly jars and arranging them on a pantry shelf.

"Bubbe, please. I need something to do."

"Go fix a toilet. Go clean a room. There are plenty of things you can do."

"But I don't want to do those things!" Ben's professional whining is rubbing off on me.

Bubbe ignores me and scoops up the empty box. I follow her out into the dining room, which the waiters are setting for lunch. "Bubbe, I promise I won't be nasty to the guests. I'm just tired. Can I please work the lunch shift?" Reuben glances at me as he places a napkin fan on a place setting. I try not to make eye contact with him, but I'm too late.

Bubbe takes my chin in her hand. "Not being nasty isn't good enough, Yussel." I wince when she uses my Yiddish name. "What happened to your Lakewood friends? Why aren't you playing with them today?"

Playing. Like I'm a four-year-old. "They had other things to do today."

She looks me over for a moment. I press a tight smile on my face. "Fine," she says. "Go help Reuben."

How awful would it be for me to tell her I'll work with anyone but Reuben right now? "Thanks, Bubbe."

I join my brother and start folding napkins without saying anything to him. He moves around a table, placing forks. After a few minutes, he leans on the back of a chair and says, "You got yourself together, squirt?"

I don't bother to correct him about the nickname. I'm too busy remaking a fan for the fifth time. "Yeah, I'm fine."

"Good." A moment later, he asks, "Why aren't you with Mel right now?"

That does it. "Mel? You don't get to call her Mel!"

He scans the room to see if anyone is looking at us. "Joey, what is your problem? What is with you lately?"

I puff my chest out, but I'm still so much smaller than he is. "You're going out with Melanie every night now?"

He runs his fingers through his curly black hair. "Joey, we're just hanging out. Nothing is going on."

"I don't believe you." I go back to folding napkins.

Reuben does something he's never done before. He snarls at me. "I don't care if you believe me! She's not your girlfriend, you know!"

Of course I know. But hearing those words out loud makes them real. And they sting. Until now, Melanie and I were suspended in our little world, where I was a different Joey, a better Joey. Reuben brought me back to this world, and it stinks. "Well, she's not yours either!" I spit back at him. *Great comeback, Joey.*

Bubbe hurries up to us and grabs both of us by the wrist. "Stop this!" she hisses. We look around, and all of the other waitstaff is staring at us, even Simon. To Reuben she says, "Set the tables!" She lets him go, and he shakes his head at me. Bubbe turns to me. "You are going to the front desk, and Uncle Sol is going to give you work to do this afternoon. Do you hear me?"

"Fine!" I stalk off, but not before I shoot Reuben a nasty scowl.

Uncle Sol isn't even at the front desk, so I go into his office and slam the door behind me. I slide down to the cold tile floor and bawl.

* * *

Uncle Sol finds me in his office, and I'm such a mess that he doesn't ask me to do anything for an hour or so. I spend the rest of the afternoon filing old papers and kicking the file cabinet. Every once in a while, Uncle Sol looks in on me and says, "You okay in here?" But I just wave him off.

The man in the expensive suit who was here a couple of weeks ago is back. I spy him through the office window at the front desk with Zeyde and Uncle Sol. The man talks and talks, and Uncle Sol moves his head around, refusing to meet the guy's eye. Zeyde rubs his forehead and offers the man a small nod every so often. My stomach churns just watching this little scene. When the man finally leaves, Zeyde notices me in the office and opens the door.

"Who's that man?" I ask. "That's the second time I've seen him here talking to Uncle Sol."

Zeyde stands in the doorway with his hands behind his back. "Your bubbe tells me that you're not feeling so good today."

He doesn't want to talk about the man in the suit. Maybe I don't either. "I'm okay," I mumble. Zeyde smiles at me, more with his eyes than his mouth. I sag against a file cabinet. All that crying earlier has given me a terrible headache.

"Come with me, Joseph. I need your help up on the fifth floor."

I exhale, long and loud. I'm not in the state of mind to fix a toilet, but at least this will get me out of the office. These walls are closing in on me. I drag myself over to my grandfather, and he claps a hand on my shoulder. He lifts his toolbox from a closet near the office, and I follow him around to the service elevator.

On the elevator, Zeyde hums a tune I've heard a million times. I think it's a song I learned when I was little. The mournful melody matches my mood.

We step out on the fifth floor, and Zeyde leads me

down the hall to one of the guest rooms. He knocks on the door. When no one answers, he unlocks the door with his master key and we shuffle inside. "This is Mrs. Taub's room," he says. "She told me that the bathtub isn't draining, so we need to unclog the drain."

Unclogging a drain is one of the more disgusting jobs Zeyde has to do at the St. Bonaventure. But we do it together, and it's not so awful. I hand Zeyde the needle-nose pliers and the long hook he's made out of a coat hanger, and he pulls up a huge, wet glob of gunk from the drain. He holds the muck up in the air by the pliers and dangles it near my face, and we both laugh like I haven't laughed in who-knows-how-long. We finish the whole operation in ten minutes. He didn't really need my help with this. I think he brought me up here to give me a distraction.

I put on some rubber gloves and scrub out the tub with a cleanser that smells like a hospital while he transfers the mound of grossness into a bag. He stands at the sink for a solid couple of minutes, washing his hands and humming. All the while, I turn things over in my mind: I'm fighting with Reuben. Melanie hates me. I'm neck-deep in lies to my family. And—how can I forget?—there's a mystery package hidden in my grandparents' house like an animal lying in wait, and I'm the one who put it there.

How am I supposed to untangle myself from all of this? Wasn't it just a few days ago that I felt so good at the synagogue? Why won't God help me out now?

Zeyde clears his throat, and I realize that I'm scouring the bathtub the way Mom scrubs a dirty oven. My eyes water up again, and I blurt out, "Zeyde, you believe in God, right? You don't even have to think about it, do you? You just believe in God."

Zeyde sits on the edge of the tub. "Asking questions is very important, Joseph, even if those questions are about God. In the Jewish faith, people are always asking questions and arguing the answers. How do you think we've become such good arguers?" He chuckles, which makes me smile a little, despite how rotten I feel. "I do believe in God. I choose to have faith that God exists. That's my choice. You'll make your choice. You're not sure that you believe in God?"

I wince. "Would you be mad at me if I wasn't sure? Wouldn't that make me a bad Jew?"

"How could I be mad at you for questioning? There are many reasons for doubting God's existence. You don't have to understand God to be a good Jew. Who truly understands God?"

Nobody, I guess. I'm not sure whether that makes me feel better or worse.

"Isn't God supposed to make everything okay?"

Zeyde raises his eyebrows at me. "Joseph, you can ask God for guidance, but what you do in your life is up to you, not God. You shouldn't go through life thinking that God will take away your daily hardships or difficulties. You can't base your faith in God on how well or how poorly your day has gone. It's not God's job to make anyone's life perfect."

"Sometimes, I feel like God doesn't care at all." The smell of the bleach must have gotten to me. My body sags against the tub. My neck can barely support the weight of my head.

Zeyde takes my chin in his hand. I sniff in the scent of Ivory soap. "You are a lucky boy, Joseph. You have your mother and father and your brothers. You have your bubbe and me and your uncle—so many people who love you. If you feel your faith is weak, your family will give you strength. Your family will help you find your faith." He leans over and kisses my forehead.

I wish I could believe him. But all those words—strength, faith, God—they're like bubbles in the air. And as soon as I get close enough to touch one of them, it pops and disappears. I wish wanting them badly enough made them real.

I hand him the scrub brush, and he packs up his tools. We're both quiet as we leave Mrs. Taub's room.

I turn to Zeyde in the elevator. "That man you and

Uncle Sol were talking to—he's from one of the casinos? He wants to buy the St. Bonaventure?"

"I don't know what he wants to do, Joseph. Right now, he just comes in and tells us all the things that are wrong with the hotel."

"Wouldn't you be sad if you sold the hotel? It's everything to you, isn't it?"

"This place? No, not at all." Zeyde sets his hand on top of my head, like he's a rabbi giving me a blessing. "You and your brothers, you are everything to me. And your bubbe and your parents and your uncle. My family is everything. The hotel is just a building."

I wonder if the rest of the family feels that way about me, if I'm part of their everything. Am I part of Artie Bishop's everything? I doubt it. Which is okay, actually, because aside from Melanie, he's not part of my everything either. Being "one of the guys" isn't the same as being part of a family.

Back in the lobby, Ben belts out a show tune. Mom sings along and claps. She's his lone audience member, but he doesn't seem to care. I sit down on the edge of the fountain, next to one of the frogs, the one I always rub when I walk through here. I've done that so much that the patina on top of its head is worn and dull. It sure is ugly.

★ ★ ★

The car ride back to Bubbe and Zeyde's house is silent. I stare at the back of Mom's head as she drives. All four of us brothers are hunkered down in our seats, peering out the windows or at anything besides one another. Mom shifts around behind the wheel, clearing her throat and using every ounce of energy she has not to pry.

We're drifting down Ventnor Avenue when Mom says, "Benjamin and I have to go to New York tomorrow and Friday. We're interviewing new agents for him. Marty Katz is retiring." No one responds.

The sky darkens, and soon, fat raindrops pelt the hood of the car like bullets.

"Mom?" It's Simon. I haven't heard his voice all day.

Mom keeps her eyes on the road. "Hmm?"

"Can you make me a grilled cheese when we get to the house? I didn't eat much today."

I wait for Mom to tell him that we just had a meat dinner, so he'll have to wait before he can have any dairy.

But after a moment, Mom says, "Sure, honey. I'll make it as soon as we get in the house."

★ ★ ★

At eleven o'clock, I'm alone in the storage room, the Hot Wheels case open in front of me. My legs buckle.

The package is gone.

CHAPTER 12

At three a.m., I'm still staring at pirate maps on my room's horrible wallpaper, just like I have been for hours.

The package is gone. Artie's package that I was supposed to keep safe is gone.

I spent an hour pulling the storage room apart, but it's not there.

Maybe I moved the package and just forgot. Maybe I was sleepwalking last night and put it somewhere else. Maybe the package ripped through the Hot Wheels case completely on its own, and it fell into a black hole in the universe.

Or maybe someone took it.

When Artie finds out, he's going to hit the roof. I have only a vague idea of what he'll do to my family and me, but if I let my mind wander, I'm sure I can come up with more details. I can't imagine Artie will cut me any slack for losing track of his precious package.

I'm too scared to cry.

This aloneness isn't like any other aloneness I've ever felt. This aloneness is a yawning, gaping pit, and I'm in the pit, and it keeps widening and widening until I'm no more than a speck on the bottom of a huge crater. And when I look up, all I see is Artie and Ralphie shoveling dirt into the pit, covering me, burying me deeper and deeper. With each scoop of dirt that he drops, Artie says, "So glad you're a part of the family, kid. So glad you're one of the guys."

Only the far-off sound of Ben's snoring breaks the dead silence of the house.

Another thought has been creeping its way up to my brain since I realized the package wasn't there. Now that thought is a lizard with sharp little claws slithering around up there in my head.

Simon took the package.

He must have found it the other night when he was messing around in the storage room, and he took it. I don't know why or what he's done with it, but there's no other explanation. He was in the storage room, and he wouldn't let me in, and it's the only thing that makes sense.

I need to get it back. I need to make this right. What other choice do I have?

★ ★ ★

Mom and Ben leave for New York City very early on Thursday morning. Reuben drives them to the bus station because Mom doesn't feel like fighting traffic and paying for parking in New York. They won't be back until Saturday at some point. That's fine with me because now there are two fewer people in the house to get in my way or ask me questions. I need to use any moments I can get alone in the house to look through Simon's stuff.

When we get in the car to drive to the hotel, Reuben, Simon, and I are a silent trio. Simon sprawls out on the back seat, which is strange because he always rides shotgun when it's just the three of us. But this week, Simon has been moodier and more sour than ever. It's as if that Monopoly game happened in another lifetime. All I want to do is shake him and scream at him, "Do you know what you've done by taking that package?" Not that he'd answer me. He'd tear my head off before Artie even gets a chance to touch me.

Reuben is behind the wheel. He turns around to look over his shoulder as he gets ready to back out of the driveway.

"Wait!" I say, and Reuben hits the brakes. He sighs the heaviest sigh I've ever heard from him.

"What is it?" he grumbles.

My mouth hangs open for a minute while I fish around in my head for some excuse to go back inside. A bubble pops in my brain: "I have to go to the bathroom, really badly."

"Come on, squirt!" Simon whines from behind me. "Just hold it until we get to the hotel!"

I turn to face him. "First of all, stop calling me that. Second of all, no. I have to, you know, *go.*"

Simon rolls his head around and groans. Reuben presses his forehead to the steering wheel. "Go!" he says. "Don't take forever, okay?"

"I won't. I'll be two minutes." I run back into the house. I don't have much time, but it's enough to take a quick look in my brothers' bedroom.

I take the stairs three at a time and bound down the hall.

It looks like Macy's exploded in their room. I could outfit an entire basketball team from the shirts and shorts sitting in mounds on the floor. A pile of pants covers the room's only chair. My eyes dart around. How am I going to find anything in this mess?

From the corner of my eye, I see a partially opened dresser drawer. I rifle through it. Socks, underwear, no package. I yank the other drawers open and root through them. Again, no package. I'm out of time. I have to get back to the car. I kick over a heap of clean, folded laundry in a corner, but there's nothing there either. I have to go. I haven't even looked in the real hiding places yet, like the closet and under the beds, but I'll have to do that later.

I dash to the car, and as soon as I'm in the seat, Simon

says, "Took you long enough. You have the runs or something?"

I heave my own sigh, and Reuben backs out of the driveway.

★ ★ ★

I'm extra cautious and attentive during the breakfast shift. Reuben side-eyes me a lot. When I tell him I'm leaving, he says, "Don't get on Melanie's case about going out with me, okay? I'm the jerk, not her."

"Oh, I know," I reply, and I turn on my heels like I'm too good to give him any more of my time. I can be a jerk too.

"Joey!" Reuben's voice is tight, and that makes me turn back to him. "Come here for a sec."

I stand in front of him and settle a defiant frown on my face.

I think he's going to tell me off or something, but he doesn't. Instead, he reaches for me and pulls me into a hug. I don't want to forgive him. I don't want to feel any comfort from him at all. But his hug cocoons me, and my anger dissolves. I hook my arms around him and squeeze, and some of his strength flows into me and calms me. He pats my back and lets me go. We don't say a word to each other. We don't have to.

I don't even bother to change before I bolt out to the Boardwalk. I have no idea what I'm going to say to Melanie, but I can't make things right with Artie until I make things right with her. I almost run headlong into an elderly couple shuffling along holding hands. I side-step them like I'm avoiding the tag at second base. My waiter shoes rub my feet with every step, and I'm pretty sure my little toes are going to start bleeding soon. But I focus on the Pinky's sign ahead of me and make it there in record time.

Ralphie and Grunts sit at the same table as the last time I saw them. But this time, they're not talking. In fact, they're not doing anything but staring off into space and dragging on cigarettes. Grunts sees me approaching and knocks Ralphie in the arm.

"Hey, Good-man," Ralphie says, his voice flat.

"Hi." I'm all business now. "Is Melanie here yet?"

Ralphie taps his ash into a black plastic ashtray. "Do I look like her father? Just go over there and have a seat and wait for her." He indicates a table in the corner with his chin.

I'm not sure why he didn't ask me to sit at their table, but he doesn't seem to be in a mood to socialize. I slump into a chair as far away from those guys as I can get. And I wait.

And I wait some more. I've never seen Ralphie be

this quiet for this long a stretch. The longer he's silent and still, the more I squirm in my chair. This isn't the Ralphie who picked me up and spun me around when I won at Skee-Ball. This is the Ralphie intimidating someone on the pay phone, the Ralphie cruising down my grandparents' street in a Caddy with blood-red seats. He's acting like a knight from *The Once and Future King*. He's all civilized on the outside, but under the surface, he's ready to go to war.

Lunchtime comes and goes. The bar fills up, and Tommy keeps looking over at me as he brings people drinks. He wants this table for paying customers. But I'm not moving.

At about one thirty, Artie comes into the room. Melanie follows a few steps behind, her head down, her face hidden by her hair. My heart hammers in my chest. They don't notice me at first. I want to jump out of my seat and run over to her. I want her to look up at me and smile and greet me like she always does: "Hey, Goodman! What're we doing today?"

She stands with her dad at the table where Ralphie now sits with Eddie. Grunts left an hour ago. She plays with her hair, holding it in a ponytail and then letting it drop around her shoulders. All I want to do is move closer to her.

I rise from my seat and will her to see me. Finally, she

turns her head toward me, and her eyes widen. I wave to her, a brief shake of my hand. She doesn't wave back, but she comes toward me, her expression unreadable. When we're eye to eye, she crosses her arms in front of her chest.

"I'm sorry about yesterday," I say. "I don't even know why I got so mad, but I was out of line."

She lets her arms fall to her sides. After a moment, she shrugs and shakes her head. "Nothing happened between Reuben and me, you know."

"It's none of my business. You were right. I'm sorry I acted like such a dope." What else can I say? There's got to be something else I can say. "I gave away the money, the twenty dollars."

"You gave it away?"

"Well, I let it blow out of my hand, and then a little girl picked it up and walked away with it."

She side-eyes me. "So you didn't actually give it away."

I shrug. "I didn't keep it."

One side of her lip curls ever so slightly. "Well, Goodman, you're not seeing that money again."

A flutter in my stomach turns into backflips. "Probably not."

Melanie fiddles with her bead bracelet. "How long have you been here waiting?"

"Long enough to watch Eddie eat breakfast, a snack,

and lunch. I thought he was going to eat the table at one point."

She laughs. The sound is like music. "If it makes you feel any better, I just spent half the day sitting in the car while my dad drove all over Atlantic City seeing his business partners. This city is really gross. There's trash everywhere and shady characters hanging out on street corners. I didn't even want to be alone in the car at half the places we pulled up to."

From across the room, Artie calls to me. "Joey! Come here!"

I swallow. The image of the missing package snaps in my head.

I edge over to Artie, and he leads me away from Ralphie and Eddie. "Joey, I'm cutting Melanie's visit short. Her mother wants her home, and I have business I need to attend to, so she's going back to Hackensack tonight."

"Tonight?" My mouth feels like it's filled with paste.

"Tonight," he says. "So, I'm going to give you your thirty bucks now. I won't even dock your pay for upsetting her yesterday, though I should."

"Artie, I don't want the money."

"What do you mean?" Artie turns me toward him so we're face to face. "You did a job for me, and I pay people who do jobs for me." He takes the wad of cash from the pocket of his trousers and starts to count.

"I don't want you to be insulted," I say. "I just don't want any money."

Artie's brows draw together. "You don't want money? Who doesn't want money?"

I shrug. I look up, right into Artie's eyes. "Is it okay if Melanie and I go for a walk? So I can say goodbye?"

Artie holds my gaze for a moment. "Sure, go ahead." I turn to go, but he calls me back. "Our business isn't over, Joey. You know what I'm talking about?" I look away and nod. *Yes, I know exactly what you're talking about. One crisis at a time, please.*

Melanie and I go out onto the Boardwalk and lean against the railing overlooking the beach. I can't believe this is the last time I'll do this with her. "You're going home tonight, huh?"

"Yeah. I wouldn't have left without saying goodbye, though. We're going to stay in touch, right?"

I squint into the sun. "Of course we are."

She props a forearm on my shoulder and leans her head toward me. "I'd really like to say goodbye to Reuben if I could. Can we go over to the hotel?"

"Sure. He'll want to say goodbye to you too."

At the St. Bonaventure, we find Reuben sitting in Uncle Sol's office with his feet propped up. He's shoveling sherbet into his mouth from a silver dish. He sees Melanie and me in the doorway and jumps up. "Hey!"

The three of us end up sitting in a row on the floor in the hallway by the ballroom, our backs against the wall. We're the only ones back here, and it's just what we need. We talk about a lot of things, and we talk about nothing. We laugh, and we joke around. Melanie asks for some sherbet, and I go off to the kitchen to find her some.

I pad back toward the hallway with a dish of lemon sherbet for Mel, and I stop before I come around the corner where they can see me. They're speaking softly to each other. "He's a good kid," Melanie is saying. "You're lucky to have him for a brother." I close my eyes and press my lips together to keep that inside me for a long moment.

Reuben says, "Joey's the best of the four of us. He doesn't realize how he holds all of us together. He's the one who makes sure everyone is okay, tries to fix things if we're not. He's always thinking about us. I'm probably going to be an accountant, like our dad, and Ben will be an actor, of course. Simon will race cars or become a Hollywood stuntman or something. But Joey . . . the sky's the limit for him. I wish he knew that about himself. I don't think he does."

At that moment, I become weightless. I float upward, buoyed by everything that's pouring from my heart. I drift over Melanie and Reuben, over the frogs in the fountain and the lounge chairs by the pool, over the St. Bonaventure and the Boardwalk and Steel Pier. I drift out over the ocean where the only sounds are the wind and the gulls and the endless break of the waves in all that brilliant blue.

* * *

"I'm going to walk back to Pinky's by myself," Melanie says a little while later.

"No, we'll walk with you," Reuben replies.

Melanie stands and stretches, so we stand too. "No, you guys stay here. I want to walk by myself."

"Your dad won't like that," I say.

Melanie elbows me in the side, and I pretend to buckle. "I keep telling you, Goodman! You don't know him. My dad's a pussycat." She stands on her tiptoes to hug Reuben. "Have a great senior year, Reuben. Don't break too many hearts."

He chuckles. "And you stay out of trouble, okay?"

She reaches for me and hugs me close. "And you— don't take everything so seriously, all right? Go laugh at the ape woman every once in a while."

I'm never going back to see the ape woman, but I get what she means, so I nod.

Melanie starts down the hallway, and we watch her

go. About halfway down, she spins around and throws a kiss, like she's a movie star. As she disappears around the next corner, she yells, "That was for you, Joey Goodman!"

I smile so broadly that it hurts. But I know where the pain is really coming from.

CHAPTER 13

Reuben and I are setting the tables for dinner when he says, "Uncle Sol's going to show a movie tonight. Simon and I are on refreshment table duty. Want to come? All the candy you can eat!"

I barely register what he's saying. Thoughts about where I can check for the package back at the house spill out of my brain. "Actually, do you mind if I skip it tonight?" If I can get him to drive me to the house, I'll have a few hours alone to search the place from top to bottom. "I'm really bummed out about Melanie. I would rather go home and get some sleep."

Reuben raises his eyebrows at me. "Joey Goodman is turning down candy? You *must* be bummed. I guess I can take you back to the house after dinner, before the movie starts."

"Thanks, Reuben," I say, and I play it up by casting my eyes down at the floor. *It's just one more lie. No big deal.* I mean, I am upset about Melanie leaving, but that's not why I want to go back to the house.

Simon looks me up and down when he hears I'm

going back early. "What are you going to do at the house?" he asks me. Simon has never cared what I do on my own time. Asking me this question at this particular moment assures me that he is hiding something.

"I don't know. I'll find something on TV." I'm disturbed by how good I'm getting at making stuff up.

Simon doesn't respond. He narrows his eyes at me, and I can practically see the cogs of his mind whirling. I want to scream at him, "This is all your fault! Everything would be fine if you hadn't taken that package!" Why does everything with him have to be so hard?

On the way to the house, Reuben chats away, but I keep my eyes on the road in front of us. He reminds me that tomorrow is Friday, so Dad will be coming down to the shore in the morning. And Mom and Ben will be back on Saturday. Just what I need. I know Zeyde said that my family will give me strength, but right now, I want to be alone.

Reuben pulls up in front of the house. "Hey, Joey?" he says after I get out of the car.

"Yeah?"

"If anything is ever bugging you, you can tell me, you know."

I chew my lip. I can't think of anything I'd gain by spilling the beans now. Reuben would be so disappointed in me. He might even tell Dad, which absolutely cannot happen. I can just picture my dad confronting Artie about everything. That wouldn't end well. Besides, I'm about to go in the house and find the missing package anyway, aren't I? My problem's about to be solved. "Thanks," I say finally. "Everything's fine."

Reuben glances at my knuckles, which are white from pulling my fists so tight. I drop my hands to my sides. But he's already seen what's what. "I'll be back later. Don't eat too much ice cream."

I force a grin on my face, wave to him, and walk toward the house. I can't look at him anymore. Or maybe I can't allow him to look at me anymore.

* * *

I turn the house upside down looking for the package. I check the storage room again and search under all the beds, even the one in my grandparents' bedroom. I ransack the closet in Simon and Reuben's room, if you can ransack something that's already a complete mess. I look in every closet, in every cabinet, behind every door. The longer I go without finding it, the more desperate I become.

"Come on!" I yell every time I yank open a drawer and the package isn't there. A cabinet in the laundry room comes off one of its hinges when I slam it closed, and I waste precious minutes looking for a screwdriver to fix it. I crawl around on the floor, looking under chairs. My hands grope the underside of every table. I even look inside the toilet tanks.

I drop onto the living room couch and put my head in my hands. *It's gone.* Whatever Simon did with the package, it's not here. I was so sure I'd find it tonight! I grip my hair and tug, wanting to pull out every strand.

Simon could have hidden the package anywhere. For all I know, he opened it and hid whatever was in it. How is it that I've never once given any thought to what the package actually contains? I have no idea what to look for. It could be important papers or money or some poor guy's nose!

There's only one thing I can do now.

When Reuben and Simon get home, I'm going to confront Simon and find out what he's done with that package. I have to. If I don't, my whole family will be right under the king of Steel Pier's thumb.

★ ★ ★

As soon as my brothers come through the doorway, I point my finger right in Simon's face. "Tell me what you did with the package you found, Simon. You'd better come clean right now!"

He squishes his eyebrows together. "What package? I have no idea what you're talking about, squirt." He tries to move around me, but I won't let him. Not this time.

"Don't lie, Simon! I need you to tell me the truth. The package is missing, and you were in the storage room the other night. Tell me what you did with it!"

Simon shoves me back, and I bang into the coat closet door. The knob hits me right on my spine. "What's wrong with you? You sound like you've lost your mind, you know that?" he says as he moves away toward the steps.

I yank the back of his shirt and pull him back. "I've searched the whole house! Where did you put it? Did you open it?"

"Open what?" He jerks away from me and straightens his shirt. "I already told you! I don't know what you're talking about." He marches upstairs. I want to scream.

Reuben runs back into the hallway from the kitchen. "What's going on out here? What's with all the yelling?"

"Forget it. Just forget it." I climb the stairs like my feet weigh a thousand pounds.

Reuben calls after me. "Joey, what's going on with you?"

But I don't answer. I just drag myself into my room and close the door. I'll have to face up to this tomorrow. I'll have to tell Artie that his package is gone, and I don't know how to get it back.

When I walk into Pinky's on Friday morning, Ralphie barely looks up from his newspaper. Grunts gets up from the table and goes off toward the back door. *Believe me*, I want to say, *I'm not thrilled about being here myself.*

Artie gives me a weak smile. "Hello, Joey. What brings you out here today?"

My shoulders curl in. "I have to talk to you."

He pulls a chair over from a nearby table and pats the seat. "What's the matter, kid?"

I sit on the edge of the chair and close my eyes. My heart beats so fast that I think it's going to explode. But now is the moment. I force the words out of my mouth. "The package is gone."

Ralphie's eyes snap up.

My lip trembles. So do my hands.

Artie leans in closer. "Joey, what do you mean, 'The package is gone'?"

"I mean, I made sure it was in a safe place in my grandparents' storage room. Ralphie even told me it was a good hiding spot, but then when I went to check on it, it wasn't there. I've looked everywhere for it, honest! It isn't anywhere in my grandparents' house. I think my brother Simon took it, but he won't tell me where it is.

I'm so sorry, Artie. I'm so sorry." I sniff in as deep as I can to compose myself.

"Your brother Simon? That's not the brother I met."

"No, you met Reuben. He's my oldest brother. Simon's a year younger than Reuben."

Artie blinks at me. "And what makes you think Simon took the package?"

"He was in the storage room the other night, and he was making all kinds of noise in there, and when I tried to see what he was doing, he wouldn't let me in. And then last night when I asked him if he had it, he pretended he didn't know what I was talking about."

Artie cracks his knuckles. "Joey, I need that package. Do you understand? If I don't get that package back, bad things will happen."

Ralphie grips his newspaper so hard it crumples in his fists.

Artie puts his hand on my shoulder. I'm starting to hate when he does that. "Joey, you're going to get the package back from your brother, and you're going to bring it to me tonight." He digs his fingers into my shoulder. "You're going to tell Simon that it's my package, and that you need to return it to me. Understand?"

"What if he still won't give it back?"

Artie smiles at me. It's a smile that doesn't reach his eyes—the scariest smile I've ever seen. "You tell Simon that's unacceptable, that I say that's unacceptable. You can do that, can't you?" I nod. "Of course you can. Everything's going to be okay, kid. You're going to get the package back, and you're going to bring it to me tonight. You'll meet me at Steel Pier at eleven thirty, and you'll give it to me, and everything will be fine."

How am I going to get to Steel Pier at eleven thirty tonight? "Isn't Steel Pier closed by then? I don't—"

"Steel Pier is where I do my business at night. You come up to the gates, and Ralphie will let you in."

"Can't I just bring it here? Later today?"

"No, you can't bring it here, Joey." His voice is a hammer, and every syllable he utters is like a nail in my chest. "You're going to give it to me in private. That's how it's going to be." He stands. I gaze up at him, and for the first time, he seems as big as Ralphie.

I can't breathe in this place anymore. I push up from the chair and run for the door.

On the Boardwalk, the heat scorches my throat and my eyes and my scalp. I didn't even recognize the man I just spoke with. That isn't the Artie I know.

Or maybe that's *exactly* the Artie I know.

Artie Bishop. Do I know any more about him now than I did two weeks ago? He's the king of Steel Pier, whatever that means. He beat a man up to get that title. He's not my father or my brother or my uncle. But I let him in. I let him flatter me and put his arm around my shoulder. I've wasted a lot of time thinking that I was one of Artie's guys, one of his family. I shouldn't have fallen for his scam. I wanted to be strong so badly, and he convinced me that I was. But might doesn't equal right. Might just makes people scared of one another.

I should have listened to the voices in my head when I first met that man. I should have had some faith in myself and the people who really love me.

Despite the heat, I race all the way back to the St. Bonaventure.

I make a beeline for Reuben as soon as I get to the dining room. He and Simon are cleaning up their breakfast tables.

"Where have you been, Joey?" he asks. "Why weren't you here for the breakfast shift?"

I lick my lips and pace back and forth like a lion in a circus cage.

Reuben places his palms flat on the table. "Joey, what's going on? Do you want me to get Dad?"

"No! Don't get Dad!" I sink into an empty chair. "Reuben, I need your help."

He sits down with me and pulls his chair close to mine. His eyes are wide, like he doesn't know who this Joey is. But I have to tell him everything.

So I do. I start with the day I met Artie, and I don't

stop until I reach this morning's meeting. At some point, Simon sits down with us, and I do a double take when I see concern written across his face. I tell them about the Skee-Ball money and Ralphie driving by the house and the days since I hid the package. By the time I'm done, the dining room has emptied out entirely, and I'm empty too.

Reuben leans heavily against the back of his chair. Simon watches him. I exhale a huge sigh that's filled with both relief, because now my lies are out in the open, and dread, because I don't like the look on Reuben's face. It's a mix of fear and utter disappointment.

"Say something!" I cry, a little too loudly. I whip my head around, hoping I didn't attract Bubbe's attention, but I don't see her.

"This is some mess you got yourself into, squirt."

"I know." I don't care that Reuben called me squirt.

Simon chews his thumbnail and stares at the carpet. All his usual bluster is gone.

"You didn't steal the package, did you?" I ask him. I know the answer before he says it.

"I swear to you, Joey, I didn't take it. I don't have it."

"Then who does?" The words come out of me like a squeak.

Simon swallows and shakes his head. "I don't know. I don't know."

I lean into Reuben, and he puts his arm around me.

"What am I going to do?" I sob. "I don't know what to do. What am I going to do . . . ?"

When I'm all cried out, I barely have enough energy left to pull myself upright. The three of us sit in silence as the minutes pass. My cheeks sting from my tears. Simon tugs at his shirt collar.

Finally, Reuben's voice snaps the stillness. "I'm going to Steel Pier with you tonight, and then you're done with Artie Bishop." I manage to lift my head and nod.

Simon straightens. "I'm going too."

"No!" Reuben says. "You need to stay home and make sure Dad doesn't catch on."

"I'm not going to just sit around while—"

"That's exactly what you're going to do, Simon. You're going to wait at home until Joey and I get back."

"But I could—"

Reuben bangs his fist on a table. "No! You're not coming. Understand?"

Simon scowls but finally mutters, "Okay."

Zeyde said that it's not God's job to make everything okay for me. He said that when my faith is running low, I should look to my family, that they'll be my strength.

I look at my brothers now, and I think I understand what Zeyde meant.

★ ★ ★

Near sunset, the hotel guests gather in the ballroom for Shabbat services and the Friday night meal. Reuben makes me attend. He tells me we should go about our night as usual. He tells me to act as normal as possible. What he doesn't tell me is what we're going to say to Artie on Steel Pier in a few hours.

Bubbe lights the Shabbat candles on the table at the front of the room. Then she shields her eyes from the flames as we all say the blessings to welcome the Sabbath. The words spill out of my mouth as I stare at the candle flames. They look like two little hands waving goodbye. Uncle Sol leads the rest of the service. Zeyde sings the prayers and songs, and I chant along, each word calling stronger than the one before.

I don't know what's going to happen later tonight, but right now, I know I'm right where I'm supposed to be.

★ ★ ★

I'm in my room, sitting on the edge of my cot. I turn the red Corvette over in my hands. Time is running out. It's nine thirty.

I must've read *The Once and Future King* twenty times, and I always thought that King Arthur was a great man who showed everyone that justice is mightier than the sword. Artie Bishop made me doubt that. He made me doubt everything I believed. Because in Artie's mind, might is better than right. It's more valuable, more important. In Artie's world, as long as you're willing to beat the other guy up, you can be the king. Artie's wrong, though. In his world, the fighting just goes on and on, and you can't even trust your best knights to stand with you.

Wait a minute . . . you can't even trust your best knights . . .

Why didn't I think of this before? There's only one other person in the world who knew where I hid that package. Only one other person who was in the house with me, who knew that our back door was unlocked and that the package was in the Hot Wheels case.

Ralphie.

Ralphie stole the package! I don't know when, and I don't know why, but I've never been more certain of anything in my life.

Ralphie is the thief.

Images fly across my mind: Ralphie and Grunts whispering, their heads close together: "He'll never see it coming." Ralphie hissing on the pay phone about doing something on his timeline and getting paid for it: "No, he doesn't suspect anything!" Ralphie drawing a diagram on a table with his finger . . .

Ralphie and Grunts have sold Artie out! They're going to stab Artie right in the back! Melanie will be crushed!

I bolt off the cot. "Reuben!"

Reuben rushes into the room. "What happened? What's the matter?"

I grab him by the arms. "Ralphie took the package. Artie's right-hand man. And that's not all . . ." The rest of the story spills out of me.

The only way I can save my family, the only way I can be strong the way I want to be strong, is by telling Artie what I know.

And I have to tell him tonight.

Dad's asleep in front of the TV by ten, so Reuben rouses him just long enough to get him upstairs and into bed. Simon's back in the storage room doing who-knows-what. He doesn't want anyone to come in there with him. Fine by me. At this point, I've been in that room enough for three lifetimes.

I sit in the living room staring at a spot on the wood-paneled wall. My foot is tapping a mile a minute. At ten forty-five, Reuben shakes me. "Time to go, Joey." He leans into the storage room and tells Simon that we're leaving.

"Now?" Simon's voice is muffled by the mostly closed door. He pokes his head out into the dining room. "Is it time already?"

Reuben nods. "We're going to park at the St. Bonaventure and sneak over to Steel Pier. We'll be back as soon as we can."

"What are you going to say to Artie?" Simon asks.

Reuben glances at me. "We'll figure it out."

On the ride from Margate to Atlantic City, Reuben says, "Explain to me why you think Ralphie has it in for Artie." I lay out all of the facts, everything I've seen and heard over the past two weeks. Reuben's eyes stay on the road. He nods a couple of times, but I'm not sure I've convinced him.

Reuben pulls the car into a spot behind the hotel and kills the engine. He turns to me on the seat. "Look, Joey, you don't know for sure if your theory about Ralphie is true. And if you're wrong, it will make the situation much worse. Just let me do the talking, okay? I don't want you to say anything." I blink at him for a moment. But eventually I nod.

I do know it's true, though. And I have to be the one to tell Artie about Ralphie. He may not believe me, but he certainly won't believe Reuben, whom he hardly knows.

This has to come from me. My family's lives depend on me. Artie's life depends on me, and that means that Melanie depends on me.

When we get out of the car, Reuben starts off into

the night, his hands at his sides, clenching into fists and releasing over and over.

The Boardwalk shuts down at eleven. If the cops find you out there after that, you can get arrested. So it's deserted when we climb the steps onto the boards. I've never been here so late at night. We stand on the top step.

The sound of running feet makes me jerk my head to the left. Two men are sprinting right toward us. I swallow a gasp of surprise. But they're already past us, racing down the Boardwalk, vanishing as quickly as they appeared. We listen to their footsteps fade into the night. Reuben's chest rises and falls in a shallow rhythm. Soon, mine does the same.

"Come on," he whispers. He moves to the left, sticking close to the darkened storefronts. The fuzzy, yellow glow of streetlamps dots the beach side of the Boardwalk, casting weak circles of light onto the boards. We stay in the shadows of the store awnings and freeze each time a noise startles us.

Mostly, though, all we hear are the waves breaking and crashing as the ocean churns under the moonlight. If I weren't so terrified, I'd say it was a really beautiful night.

Steel Pier rises up over the beach ahead of us. The signs along the south side of the pier are a patchwork of colored lights against the dark roofs of the long, low buildings. Empty rolling chairs stand like sentries at the pier entrance.

We stop in front of a phone booth across the boards from the pier. "Do you have a dime?" I ask.

Reuben nods. "Did you bring one in case I forgot?" I reach into my pocket, and my hand comes out with a roll of dimes. Reuben almost laughs. "From the tzedakah drawer?"

I pull out another roll from my other pocket. "I figure I'm a charity case at this point."

"Makes sense to me. Let's make that phone call." And he does.

We dash across the Boardwalk to the pier side and approach the iron gate that's stretched across the walkway.

"Do we knock?" My whisper cuts the air like an ax.

"I don't know. I—"

Ralphie appears on the other side of the gate, his cigarette lighting half of his creased face. I knew he'd be the one to meet us, but coming face-to-face with him drowns me in dread. He says nothing but slides the gate open just enough for us to squeeze through onto the pier.

Ralphie strolls ahead of us and doesn't look back. He knows we're right behind him. A pulse of fear pumps through me. I shiver, breathing hard. Reuben glances at me, and his eyes beg me to stay quiet.

Ralphie marches us through the darkened main cor-
ridor of the pier. Grimy windows spread just enough
moonlight for us to make our way through to the other
end of the long building. We exit onto the far end of the
pier, the part that stretches over the ocean, where Melanie and I watched that pitiful fight just last week. Ralphie stops and throws down his cigarette butt, crushing
it beneath his shoe. All around us, the ocean thunders.

Artie moves out of the shadows to stand a few feet
away from us to our left. To our right, Ralphie cracks
his knuckles and juts out his chin. A trickle of icy sweat
winds down my back. Reuben's eyes dart around. We're
cornered animals.

"Where's the package, Joey?" Artie yells so we'll
hear him over the roll of the waves.

Reuben pushes me behind him. "We don't have it.
It's gone."

Artie gazes out into the night for a moment. "I'm
very unhappy right now, Joey. I'm very disappointed in
you. You were supposed to get the package back from
your brother."

Reuben shakes his head. "Simon didn't take it. He
doesn't have it."

Artie leans into Reuben and pokes him hard in the
chest. "I'm not talking to you. I'm talking to Joey!"
Artie tilts his head and frowns at me. "You going to hide

behind your big brother all night, huh? You going to hide behind him and cry?"

I step forward and lock eyes with Artie. "No, Artie. I'm not going to cry. You can't make me cry. You can't make me do anything anymore. I'm not one of your guys anymore. In fact, I never was."

"Joey!" Reuben hisses, and he tries to pull me back. I don't budge.

"And you know what else?" I continue. "You were wrong about *The Once and Future King*. You were wrong about King Arthur. It's not the strongest who always come out on top."

"Really?" Artie says. "That's sure how it is in my world." Ralphie chuckles at this.

I side-eye Ralphie for a moment but quickly turn back to Artie. "In your world, no one comes out on top because the fighting never ends. No one wins, not even you. Not even the mighty king of Steel Pier."

Artie glares at me, his nostrils flaring. "Who do you think you are, talking to me like this?"

"I know exactly who I am," I say as I lift my chin. "I'm a Goodman."

Reuben draws me back and tightens his grip on my arm. "We'll pay you back." His voice quavers. "Whatever the package was worth. We'll give you whatever you want."

"I don't want your money," Artie barks. "I want that package. If your brother didn't steal it, then who did?"

I have to say it! I crush my eyes closed. *Now, Joey!*

"It was Ralphie!" I say. "Ralphie took the package!"

Ralphie's mouth twists. "Shut up, kid! Shut up right now!"

"And he's planning something, Artie! He's been planning against you for weeks! He—"

Ralphie growls like a wild dog and lunges at me. I flinch and reel back, my breath gone.

A shadow swoops down and latches onto Ralphie's back.

The shadow is Simon, and he howls like a demon. For a moment, Ralphie folds forward. But he's just too big. He tosses Simon aside like an empty soda can, and Simon's head and shoulder slam into the metal railing of the pier with a sickening crack. He drops to the ground, unmoving.

I cry out, "Simon!" Reuben lunges toward him, then freezes. If he goes to Simon, he can't protect me.

But I don't need his protection anymore.

I whip around to face Artie. "Artie, I know it's true! Ralphie took the package, and he's working with some guy named Al to hurt you! Maybe even kill you!"

Moonlight glints off something in Ralphie's hand. *A knife!* Ralphie raises his arm. Grunts emerges from the shadows like a ghost. He has a knife too! They move toward Artie.

"You had to know this was coming, Artie," Ralphie spits. Sweat glimmers on his forehead. "Even you can't be king forever."

Artie thrusts his hands out in front of him. *I have to do something!*

Melanie's face is all I see as I reach in my pockets and yell, "Noooo!"

CHAPTER 14

I hurl a roll of dimes at Ralphie's face. It thuds against his temple, and his neck snaps to the side. I fling the other roll at Grunts and hit him right in the eye. Both rolls break open, and dimes fly in their faces. They're distracted just long enough for me to yell, "Run, Artie!"

Artie turns to flee as Ralphie and Grunts raise their knives again.

A roar of motorcycles and sirens surges at us. Blazing lights flash in Ralphie's face, and voices yell, "This is the police! Drop the knives, and get your hands up! Now!"

Our phone call! It worked!

Ralphie and Grunts spin on their heels and bolt into the darkness. All that's waiting for them in that direction is the end of the pier and beyond that, the endless ocean.

Cops race by us to catch them.

Reuben is next to me in a split second. "Joey! Joey! Are you all right?"

"Yeah, I'm okay," I say. "But Simon . . ."

Reuben and I rush over to our brother and kneel next to him. He groans, and I let out a gasp of relief that he's alive. Reuben tells him not to move, that an ambulance will be here soon.

Minutes later, two men lift Simon onto a gurney.

A police officer holds a flashlight to Reuben's face. "Are you the ones who called us, son?"

Reuben winces at the light. "Yeah, that was us."

"You did the right thing."

Reuben gives me a knowing grin. "It was Joey's idea."

"You're a brave young man, Joey," the cop says. I've still got tears in my eyes, but . . .

Maybe I am.

They roll Simon into the ambulance and tell us where they're taking him. "You two should get looked at too. You're both pretty shaken up," the driver says to Reuben and me before they pull away toward the Boardwalk.

The policemen swarm around us, asking us questions and speaking into walkie-talkies. Reuben tries to push them back. "We're not saying anything right now! We need to get our dad!"

A voice crackles over the static of a walkie-talkie at a police officer's hip. Some cops have cornered Ralphie and Grunts at the end of the pier. I press my eyes closed and say thanks to something, to someone, God or otherwise.

Artie elbows his way through the circle of people surrounding me. "Joey, what you did . . . you saved my life."

"I didn't do it for you," I say. "I did it for Melanie." Reuben hugs me to him and leads me away, and I know I'll never see Artie Bishop again.

The police lead us through a door into the eerie silence and blackness of the pier buildings, and we walk down the center of Steel Pier, toward the Boardwalk. It's dark all around us, but a police officer hands us a flashlight, so Reuben holds it out, illuminating a path for us.

I think about Mom and Dad and my brothers and Uncle Sol. I think about Bubbe and Zeyde and the guests at the St. Bonaventure Hotel.

And I think about Melanie. For a couple of weeks, we ruled the Boardwalk. She was a princess and I was a prince, and that time will always be ours.

"Watch your step," Reuben says as he guides me around a trash can. "It's so dark, isn't it?"

But the Boardwalk and the hotel and our family are out there. I lift my head and smile. "I think I see some light."

★ ★ ★

Simon has a serious concussion and a broken collarbone. The doctor says he'll have to stay in the hospital for a few days to make sure he's okay. Dad's allowed to sleep in the hospital room because Simon's only sixteen. Dad says wild horses couldn't drag him away.

Mom and Ben arrive at the hospital on Saturday morning after taking the earliest bus out of New York that they could. "Mom cried the whole way here," Ben says. He pats Simon's arm. "You don't look so bad. Hey, if any reporters come by, just let me handle the press, okay?"

Simon is weak from the injuries and the pain medication, but he grins at Ben. "They're all yours, Beans."

Mom drapes herself across Simon's hospital bed and sobs. "How could this happen?" she asks through her tears. "How could someone do this to my baby?"

Simon groans, and Mom pops up. "Am I hurting you?"

"Yeah. Everything hurts."

Mom gasps. "You need more aspirin! Call the nurse!" She flies out of the room, yelling, "Nurse? Nurse? Why can't I get a nurse over here?"

Uncle Sol stands at the end of the bed and flips through Simon's medical chart. "Hmph," he says as he turns the pages. "Hmph, hmph, hmph." I'm pretty sure Uncle Sol doesn't understand a thing he's reading. "Well, young man, this is a fine way to get out of your waiter duties." He winks at Simon.

Bubbe takes Simon's hand and rubs it against her cheek. Simon lets her, which makes me smile. Maybe it's all the medication he's got in him.

* * *

Mom is dry-eyed and determined the next day.

"Okay, everybody leave," she says as she takes a seat on the edge of Simon's bed. She swishes her hand in the air at all of us. "I'm going to talk to my son alone."

Outside the room, I watch the two of them through the glass panel on the door. Mom holds Simon's face in her hands, and for the first time since all of this happened, he starts to cry. Mom hugs him and rocks him back and forth, and Simon leans his head into her and cries out as much of his pain as he can.

* * *

Farrah comes by for a few minutes on Simon's last day in the hospital. She tries to smile at him, but there's still a shadow of sadness around her.

Simon takes a big envelope from the drawer of the table near the bed and hands it to her.

She doesn't say much. She and Simon just look at each other and she strokes his arm. When she leaves, Simon turns his head away from the door, his eyes glassy.

Later, I ask him, "What was in that envelope you gave Farrah?"

Simon's eyes are closing. He's drowsy from being in this bed for so long. "I made her a collage of all the stuff we did together. Ticket stubs, pictures from the photo booth, stuff like that. I asked Reuben to bring it down here yesterday because I knew she'd be coming by."

"That's what you were doing in the storage room!" I blurt out. "You were making a present for Farrah, and you didn't want any of us to see it!"

"Well, it's kind of cheesy."

I shake my head. "I think it's really cool. Did you two break up?"

Simon gets quiet for a minute. "She's going to live with her mom in California. At least she'll be away from her dad."

After a moment, I say, "There's something I've been meaning to ask you."

"Oh, yeah? What's that, squirt?"

"Why did you follow Reuben and me to Steel Pier that night?"

"Don't you know me by now?" he says with a sleepy smirk. "Did you think you could leave the house to meet up with some dangerous gangster and *not* have me follow you? As soon as you and Reuben closed the door behind you, I grabbed Dad's car keys. I caught up with you in the hotel parking lot and followed you from there." He coughs, and pain slides across his face for a moment.

I pull up close to the bed. Simon can barely stay awake. "I'm glad you're my brother, Simon."

"Me too, squirt," he mumbles. "Me too." I watch him drift off to sleep, and in my head, I say a prayer for him—for all of us.

*   *   *

It's our last day at the hotel. August is over, and school will be starting soon. Bubbe gives all of us kisses on the crowns of our heads, and she tries to hug all four of us at once. She speaks softly in Yiddish as she squeezes our cheeks.

"Where's Zeyde?" I ask.

Bubbe smiles at me. "He's in the tearoom, bubbeleh."

I don't see Zeyde when I first enter the room. Guests fill many of the knotty wood tables and spindly chairs, and I can hear them chatting and squabbling and complaining. It all makes me smile.

From somewhere to my left comes Zeyde's hushed voice: "Joseph." He's standing by a wall of framed photographs and postcards that I haven't looked at in years.

He stands with his hands behind his back, peering at the pictures through his glasses. He looks like he's listening to someone speak to him in a language he doesn't understand. "Hi, Zeyde," I say, my voice barely above an office whisper.

Zeyde doesn't look at me but points to one of the old photos. It's a vintage poster of Steel Pier like the one that was hanging in poor Mrs. Goldberg's room, only this one shows Steel Pier at night. A perfect, round moon hangs high over the pier like a prop in an old-time movie. It's shadowy on the Boardwalk, but Steel Pier glows with colored lights, from its arcaded entrance all the way to its farthest edge, a half mile out to sea.

Next to me, Zeyde says, "In its day, there was nothing like Steel Pier, here in Atlantic City or anywhere else. A wonderland . . . a marvel . . ." He sighs. "In March of 1962, a storm tore up the pier. Your bubbe and I saw a barge cut right through it, here." He runs a finger across the far end of the pier like a saw cutting through his thoughts. "What a storm . . ."

Zeyde shuffles over to another frame farther down the wall. This one holds a full-color St. Bonaventure Hotel postcard. "I found this in your uncle's office the other day. I think we had all forgotten about it. Look, Yussel." He takes it off the wall and shines up the glass with his shirt sleeve.

The postcard is divided into sections: four small squares, each showing a different area of the hotel, and a fifth, larger section showing the whole place, which looks like it was taken by someone hovering over the ocean.

Zeyde points to the part of the postcard displaying

the indoor pool and taps on a figure in the foreground. "That's your mother," he says, and when I look closer, I see that it is Mom, standing next to the pool in a striped bathing suit. Her hair is long and frizzy, and she looks so young. Zeyde points to two tiny dots of color, which I see are people in the pool. "That's Reuben and Simon." He draws their names out as he indicates each one. Next to the pool, a man sits in a green, plastic chair with a dark-haired baby on his lap.

"Is that me and Dad?" I ask, awed.

Zeyde squints harder and lets out a shaky laugh. "Yes! That is little baby Yussel on his papa's lap." He moves his index finger to a different section of the postcard, this one showing the lobby. The fountain and the frogs are polished and gleaming. "And see in this one," he continues, "there is your Uncle Sol and me." They stand near the fountain shaking hands, like Uncle Sol is greeting a guest.

"And there's Bubbe!" I say when I find her leaning over a table of guests in the picture of the dining room. "Wow, the hotel looks perfect in every picture."

Zeyde gestures to a table. "You have some time before you have to go? Sit and have tea with your zeyde, Yussel." He lowers himself into a chair and places the framed postcard on the table. "Sit, sit." I settle into the chair next to him.

One of the waiters comes over to us. "What can I get you, Mr. Broder?" Zeyde asks for tea for both of us, and even though I don't really want any, I am not about to say anything that might damage this little cocoon that he's nestled us in. He doesn't say a word now; he focuses on his weathered hands as he spreads them across the tabletop. Those hands have held hammers and brooms and suitcases and the Torah and his children and his grandchildren. Someday, maybe they'll hold his great-grandchildren.

The waiter returns soon with the clear carafes of hot water and two glass mugs. Zeyde dunks a tea bag into the carafe, and we watch the amber tendrils of tea spread and turn the water a deep garnet red. He drops in three sugar cubes, and they dissolve in the steaming water.

"We're selling the St. Bonaventure, Joseph."

I open my mouth to speak, but I don't know what to say. So I just listen.

"Bubbe and Uncle Sol and I have decided. The time for the casinos is coming. Our time here is over."

I think I know what he means.

"We're going to keep the frogs from the fountain for you boys. One for each of the Goodman brothers."

"I'd love that," I say.

Zeyde takes my hand in his. He sips his tea and motions for me to make mine, which I do one-handed because I don't want to move the hand he's holding. I'm surprised by how comfortable it feels to hold my grandfather's hand.

An intense silence vibrates in the air around us. It makes me smile and shiver. We both sit and drink our tea for a good long while. My gaze drifts to the postcard again. Zeyde points at one of the scenes and tells me another story about our family from a long, long time ago.

AUTHOR'S NOTE

In this book, I make Atlantic City sound like a seedy, crumbling place in the 1970s, and in some ways, that's certainly what it was. Atlantic City had been a glamorous, exciting vacation destination up until the 1950s. But as air travel became faster and more affordable, people started traveling with their families to new, faraway places. By the '70s, Atlantic City's best days were in the past, as local businesses that had relied on tourism struggled to survive.

But I wasn't aware of any of that at the time. I was a little girl whose grandparents owned the stately St. Charles Hotel on the Boardwalk. My brother and my cousins and I had the run of the place, and it was a wonderland to me. My parents were always getting dressed up and going to dinner-dances and parties in the ballroom. I used to sneak into the huge kitchen when I was hungry, and the staff would cut open those little wax paper-lined boxes of cereal for me and pour the milk right into the box. Out on the Boardwalk was Steel's Fudge and James'

Salt Water Taffy. My brother and I played Skee-Ball and pinball to our hearts' content at the arcades. I loved to shake the gift shops' Atlantic City snow globes and watch as the "sand" settled on the tiny beach scenes inside the plastic domes. We visited Steel Pier and Million Dollar Pier and rode the Tilt-A-Whirl and the Himalaya all afternoon. To me, Atlantic City was magical.

When casino gambling became legal in Atlantic City, everything changed. Sure, the glamour was back, at least inside the casinos, but the Boardwalk lost its allure for me. The family-owned hotels that had dotted the Boardwalk for so many years were demolished to make way for the casinos. The St. Charles Hotel was among the casualties. The hotel I loved—with the lobby fountain's four water-shooting frogs, the tearoom where my mother played mah-jongg, and the heavy revolving door that led out onto the Boardwalk—was gone.

But my big Jewish family remained. For many more years, we'd go down the shore to Bubbe and Zeyde's house for brunch and to Aunt Adele and Uncle Danny's house for Passover seders. My cousin Gail and I continued to put on little plays for anyone who'd watch them. I still remembered all the fun of the St. Charles, but it had been, in fact, just a building. For every bar mitzvah or bat mitzvah, wedding, and Jewish holiday, we still gathered to eat, laugh, and argue! The Atlantic City that

I knew when I was young—the Boardwalk, Steel Pier, the St. Charles Hotel—would live on in my memories, but it was in one another that my family found strength and love.

I still have this postcard from the St. Charles Hotel. It was produced in 1967 or 1968, and in it I see Bubbe and Zeyde, Aunt Adele, Uncle Danny, my cousins Gail and Laura, my mother, my brother, and even me, just a baby sitting on my father's lap by the pool. The postcard is precious to me, not because it shows the St. Charles Hotel, but because the people in it are my family, and I love them all.

ACKNOWLEDGMENTS

I've dreamed of being a writer since I was six years old. I think I finally am one. And now I get to say thank you to the wonderful people who guided me and mentored me and cheered me on and believed in me, and I'm grateful to each and every one of you.

Thank you to Rena Rossner, my Wonder Woman agent who, I swear, never sleeps. Thank you for turning this manuscript away the first time I sent it to you, and thank you for falling in love with it the second time around. You are my champion.

Thank you to Amy Fitzgerald, my editor, who has the patience of a saint. You calmly answered every question, solved every problem, and reassured me at every turn. Thanks also to Joni Sussman at Kar-Ben Books for seeing something special in this story and to the rest of the Lerner team, including Danielle Carnito and Erica Johnson, and to cover artist Alisha Monnin. Many thanks to everyone at PJ Library and PJ Our Way for their support for me and so many other Jewish writers. Jewish kids need to see themselves in the books they read, and your generosity ensures that our community will not be sidelined and silenced.

Erik Kraft, you are a fantastic writing teacher, and you really made me believe this was something I could do. Thank you. A huge thank-you to Cindy Baldwin and Amanda Rawson-Hill and everyone at Pitch Wars, including the Class of 2018. Cindy and Amanda, you are the best mentors an old girl could ever have, and I am in awe of your talent and grace. And lots of love to all the Team Mascara Tracks gals. TMT forever!

I am grateful to Nora Raleigh Baskin for her friendship and for not letting me give up. Thanks also to Chris Baron, Chris Tebbetts, Sarah Aronson, and Loree Griffin Burns, who have been generous with their time and have helped me immensely. I cannot say enough wonderful things about my amazing critique group: Jane Barron, Sally Suehler, and Jerry Warmuskerken. I feel very lucky that Inked Voices brought us together. Thanks to Shannon Balloon and Pamela Thompson McCloud for reading early drafts and not telling me to burn the whole thing. And hugs to the #22Debuts!

I have amazing friends who have been with me for every step of this journey, and I will never be able to thank them enough: Bryan Miller, Peggy Sutton, Suzanne Ritter, Pat Killoren, Joyce Simson, Cindy Zive, Whitney Eads, Amy Seymour, Susan Carter, and Gwen

Nzimiro. Muchas, muchas gracias to my favorite chica and chavera, Marjorie Prince—how are you, my friend? And to the marvelous, glittery Michelle Platt, Statler to my Waldorf, there aren't enough ways to thank you.

My love for my big Jewish family knows no bounds. My parents, Barbara and Gary Kanalstein, always made me feel like I could accomplish anything. Mom and Dad, I love you both so very much. I'm grateful to Aunt Adele, Uncle Howard, and Aunt Joanne for their unconditional love all these years. My brother, Eric, and his family—Esmera, Eliyar, and Elham: I adore you all, and I'm so thankful to have you in my life. And Simeon, I'm grateful that you're now part of our family too.

Jack and Margot, thank you for inspiring me to take on the challenge of writing a book. You both believed in me more than I believed in myself. No matter how many books I end up writing, raising you will always be my proudest achievement.

Finally, Richie, you will always be the love of my life and my best friend. So I've got that going for me. Which is nice.

About the Author

Stacy Nockowitz has been a middle school educator for many years, both as a language arts teacher and as a school librarian. She is an unrepentant Jersey girl from Exit 4 on the NJ Turnpike and an outstanding Jewish mother to her grown kids, Jack and Margot. She lives in central Ohio with her husband, Richie, and their perfect cat, Queen Esther. *The Prince of Steel Pier* is her debut novel.